"I make a noose," he said. "It works fast. And permanent. Not even much kickin'."

"Big one kicked some," Jim Scarlet muttered. "Little one snapped his neck like a twig."

Willie felt a fire rage within him as they went on drinking and laughing.

"They'll know who did it," Thad Scarlet complained. "Nobody but us runs that SCAR brand."

"Knowin's just fine," Jim replied. "Provin's another thing."

The others laughed their agreement. Then Marshal Wade Maddock appeared on the road.

"Hold real still, friends," the marshal warned. "I got some men with me less than friendly."

"Run!" the shaggy man screamed as he tossed the jug aside and leaped to his feet. He got three steps before a shotgun blast from the woods threw him to the ground.

NORTH
OF
ESPERANZA

G. Clifton Wisler

FAWCETT GOLD MEDAL • NEW YORK

For Sally,
my Brazos friend

CHAPTER 1

North of the Clear Fork and south of the Salt Fork of the Brazos River, Texas was an empty, forlorn sort of place. Except for occasional stands of scrub cedars or stunted willows, only clumps of buffalo grass and prickly pear disputed ownership of the rock-strewn hills and washed-out ravines. It was a lonely land. The wind whined tormented melodies by night. By day the sandy landscape baked itself hard and unyielding. Plants yellowed, withered, and died. So did those men who tried to scratch out a living in the barren soil.

The Spaniards called that country Llano Estacado, the staked plains, for here a man dared not rely on landmarks to trace his path. Look north, south, east, or west, and the view was much the same. So they drove their stakes into the earth and prayed fortune would send them home from the unforgiving land. They called the long, flat-topped hills *mesas* and the dry beds where water once flowed became *arroyos*. Yes, they left their words, those Spaniards. From their abandoned livestock came the longhorn cattle and mustang ponies. As for the men, they survived only in the tales of golden cities and iron-headed strangers spun beside a cowboy's midnight campfire.

1

Willie Delamer knew those stories. And others besides. For that desolate country had been a home of sorts for him, and it promised to become one again.

As he knelt beside the shallow waters of the Clear Fork and stared at the face reflected in the river, he wondered what strange mischance could have brought him back to Texas, to these hills where he'd hunted buffalo as a raw-boned fourteen-year-old. Beneath his sweat-soaked cotton shirt were scars left by Yank sabers and Sioux lances. Bullets, too. Yes, lots of bullets.

He stared into the icy, steel-blue eyes that danced on the surface of the river. It wasn't pain that had made them cold and hard. The wrinkles etched in what forehead emerged from beneath a shaggy mane, bleached yellow by the sun, had been carved there by years of turmoil, torment, and killing. His fingers, even as they nervously tapped his brass buckle, seemed ready to grip the handle of a Colt pistol and deal out death.

What was it that brought a man to such a trail? What choked the joy and warmth from life and left only bitterness and regret?

"I don't know," Willie told those haunted eyes. As he gazed at the lanky, weathered figure before him, he found it hard to accept that even here, along the banks of his beloved Brazos, he was lost.

Up in the Black Hills three long years before, an old medicine man had spoken to him. What were the words? Nothing's ever so lost you can't find it? Something like that. If only a man were to go back and search where he'd lost the fool thing. But how could a man locate a soul? Hope? Dreams? Those were items too precious to be rediscovered. The dust of too many years had buried them.

He might have gone on brooding away half the morning had not the sound of horses splashing their way across the river stolen his attention.

Willie wasn't a man to like surprises, and visitors were few and far between on the Clear Fork. He stepped away from the river and fetched a Winchester rifle from his gear. As the riders came closer, he picked out three faces behind the spray. Their leader was a curly-haired boy of eighteen whose clear, eager eyes were always a wonderment to Willie. How anyone raised on hard times could retain a good humor was amazing! The other riders were a bit younger, straw-haired and weathered as Willie himself was.

"Found you!" the dark-haired boy announced as he pulled his horse to an abrupt halt.

"No need for the rifle, Major," a second boy declared. "It's Lewis Slocum. And Lamar," he added, nodding toward the dark-haired brother beside him. "Ain't changed that much in two months, have we?"

"Ain't been two months since you seen me, has it, Uncle Wil?" the youngest of the trio, Mike Cobb, called. "Was only Saturday you was at our place celebrating my birthday."

Willie couldn't help smiling. The three young men climbed down from their saddles and set about ransacking the camp in search of food. They finally located a flour sack filled with jerked venison. As they helped themselves, Willie placed a coffeepot on the embers of his morning cook fire.

"How many horses you got ready to sell?" Lamar asked.

"How many you want to buy?" Willie asked in turn. "Gone and decided to head up your own drive to Kansas this summer?"

"Pa'd skin him first," Lewis said, laughing at the notion.

"Lamar, I promised your pa fifteen," Willie told them. "And Trav's already got his six," Willie added, nodding toward young Mike.

"Sure, but last time I rode out here, you had close to thirty," Lamar noted. "You had a few penned up in that draw out Goose Creek way, too."

"You need more'n fifteen?" Willie asked. "I got another dozen maybe I'd sell."

"Ain't for us," Lamar explained. "Oh, we'd take one or

3

two over, and you know it, but wasn't that sent us out lookin' for you. It's this."

Lamar drew out a large handbill and passed it around the fire. Willie held it up and read the neatly printed letters.

HORSE AUCTION

A HORSE AUCTION will be held first Saturday of each month at WALIN'S STORE from ten o'clock in the morning until all stock is sold. All sellers welcome. Buyers by invite only.

"Man could make a fine profit auctionin' off his horses," Lewis declared, scratching his chin.

"At Walin's store?" Willie asked, laughing. "Ain't a dozen men pass through there 'fore summer."

"Used to be sparse, I'll admit," Lamar agreed. "But they gone and made 'emselves a town there now. Throckmorton. Named the county the same thing. Been wagons cartin' lumber up there lately. 'Sides the store and eatin' house, they got a blacksmith and a real saloon. Buildin' a courthouse and a jail, too. Must be twenty, thirty people by now."

"Don't sound like folks that'd buy range ponies," Willie grumbled.

"The blacksmith wants horses to hire out," Mike explained. "Told Pa that. Then there's the Scarlet brothers. They got a ranch up north a bit. Some farmers on past the Scarlets. Got a town halfway to the Salt Fork. Call it Esperanza."

"Mexicans?" Willie asked.

"Iowa farmers," Lewis answered. "Educated, though. We met some of 'em last year comin' back from Dodge City."

"Mostly women and kids to begin with," Lamar added. "Come west after the war. Most 'o the women got 'emselves widowed at Chickamauga, as I heard it. The older one's grown up now, and a few's married up and hatched little ones. Not many men about, least not as I'd say."

4

"Plenty o' girls, though," Lewis said, grinning. "Lamar and I go up there for plantin' dances. Fair to look at, them gals."

"And pitiful few skirts on the Clear Fork," Lamar lamented. "Anyhow, I expect some o' them Esperanza farmers'll want horses."

"First Saturday's only two days away," Willie noted. "Not much time to ready a string."

"That's why we rode out," Mike said. "Thought to give you a hand."

"Seems to me you got cows to round up," Willie pointed out.

"We do," Lewis admitted. "But way I see it, we go ahead and get the horses down to Pa, let him pick out his string, and you take the rest to Throckmorton and sell 'em off. Wouldn't be anything to hold you out here that way. You could help run in the longhorns and join the trail drive north."

"I been to Kansas," Willie muttered. "Ain't much to the place save bad memories."

"Be good company along the way, though," Lewis argued. "And if trouble happened along, I don't think I'd mind havin' Major Wil Delamer handy."

"Ain't been major anything in a long time," Willie insisted as he pulled the boiling coffeepot from the coals and poured four cups of muddy liquid. "Nor a Delamer, either. But I wouldn't chase company away. Don't suppose it'd be too bad seein' a new town gettin' born."

"Somethin' to tell my grandkids," Lewis boasted.

"Grandkids?" Lamar cried. "You ain't even shavin' yet, Lewis. Ain't likely you'll have any grandkids."

The Slocum brothers set to grappling. Mike fought to restore peace and wound up in the middle of them. Willie shook his head and stepped clear of their dust. He'd been much the same. . . . Once, a very long time ago.

5

CHAPTER 2

Somehow, amid the pranking and foolishness, they got twenty horses delivered to Ted Slocum's ranch downriver and drove a dozen others to Throckmorton in time for Saturday's auction.

"Never saw them boys to hurry 'emselves like that before," Slocum observed when he shook hands on the deal. "Major, you put a shotgun to their ears or somethin'?"

"Might be a thing to try," Willie noted. "But I think it's a skirt up that way that's got 'em all lathered."

"Could be," Slocum said, cracking a grin. "I've known 'em to sneak off a time or two, and the tracks always turn north."

"Guess it's the season."

"Lord, Major, when you're that age, it's always the season. Who knows? Maybe they got a big sister wouldn't shy from a dusty ole rebel like yourself."

"Left that trail behind a lifetime ago," Willie declared as he turned toward his big gray. " 'Sides, they hail from Iowa. Not too likely to smile on a fellow who wore the gray."

"I expect they've gotten used to 'em, bein' in Texas

6

awhile. You see them fool boys stay clear o' shotgun-totin' papas, won't you?''

"Do my best," Willie said, raising his right hand and grinning at his old friend.

"And hurry on back here. We got a trail herd to put together."

Willie offered a mock salute and mounted his horse. Moments later he was leading the young Slocums and Mike Cobb north and west along the Clear Fork of the Brazos. Twelve range ponies hurried along before them.

Throckmorton proved to be much as the boys had described. Where before Stu Walin's little trading post had stood starkly alone on the broad prairie, there were now a pair of structures on either side and the skeletons of three others rising nearby. Close to fifty people had gathered around a rope corral behind Walin's store. Willie motioned his companions that way, but Lamar Slocum was already driving the lead ponies in that direction.

"Ain't little boys anymore," Willie muttered under his breath as he watched Lewis cut off a straying mustang and drive the animal along through a narrow gap in the corral's rope sides. Little Mike Cobb slapped a laggard roan mare along with a rope's end, and the last of the horses finally galloped into the corral.

"All yours now, Uncle Wil," Mike called, grinning at his young friends. "Shoot, you might's well've stayed home and had Saturday supper with Pa and the little ones."

"Might as well have," Willie said. "Long as you three figure you're up to doin' the dickerin'. I expect top price, of course. You'd surely make up any differences out o' your own pockets."

"Now hold on," Mike cried as Willie turned his horse away from the corral. "Wasn't that I was meanin'. You know I got no head for doin' business. I'm just fifteen, after all."

7

"That all?" Willie asked, halting his retreat. "And here I thought to hear you talk maybe you was figurin' to drive Trav's cows all the way to Kansas by yourself. Don't need any old-timers around."

Lewis and Lamar smiled at Mike's discomfort, and Willie took a turn at them as well. A well-aimed jest found its mark, and Lamar howled a complaint.

"Fine gratitude that is!" the eighteen-year-old objected. "Come all the way up here to help you get your horses sold, and all you can do is . . ."

"That what brought you?" Willie asked. "And I thought it was to eye those pretty farm girls over yonder."

The girls glanced shyly in Lamar's direction, and the slight-shouldered young man reddened with embarrassment. Soon Stu Walin announced it time to begin the auction, and Willie dismounted, tied off his horse on a handy hitching post, and left the youngsters to their own business. In no time Lewis located a pair of pretty straw-haired farm girls in their mid-teens. Lamar and Mike drifted over to Walin's store and struck up a conversation with three others.

"Howdy, Wil," Walin said, greeting Willie with a nod. "The whole twelve yours?"

"Every one," Willie replied.

"Plan to sell the lot?"

"If my price's met."

"Will be," a farmer called.

"I'll want plenty for the black mare," Willie explained. "Roan, too. That black-eared pinto's the best o' the lot. I won't accept . . ."

"Leave me to fetch a fair price," Walin insisted. "I'd wager you'd take less'n I'll get every time."

"Oh?" Willie said, raising an eyebrow.

"Sure," Walin explained with a grin. "You got too soft a heart for real horse tradin'. How many times've I seen you offer a good cuttin' horse to some half-starved cowboy? And what about those grays you sold Widow Schubert summer 'fore last?"

8

Young Tom Walin and another youngster nodded know-
ingly, and Willie laughed. In truth he melted under the hungry gaze of women and little ones. He shrugged his shoulders
and left Walin to commence the sale. Besides Willie's dozen
range ponies there were two good plow teams, three mules,
and a scraggly nag or two brought in by the farmers up north.
The mules and nags found a cold reception, with the blacksmith, Isaac Cummings, outbidding a skinny farm boy each
time. The plow horses brought out a brisker trade, for good
farm stock was in short supply west of Fort Worth.

Once those animals had been led out of the corral by their
new owners, Walin called for bids on the roan mare. She
wasn't as fleet as the black, but her lines were good, and
Willie'd been half-tempted to hold her back for breeding. A
tall cowboy named Wade Maddock topped all offers at
eighty dollars, and Walin announced the mare sold.

"Next up's this black," Walin shouted. "Look at her,
folks, 'cause you won't find her equal for a hundred miles."

"You said that about the roan, Stu!" Cummings shouted.

"Well, it's the truth," Walin argued. "Two fine horses.
Gentled by the best hand with horses on the Brazos,
too. Wil, what name you usin' this month?"

"Fletcher," he answered to a chorus of laughter. Most of
the old hands knew better. Three or four, like Travis Cobb
and Ted Slocum, had soldiered with Wil Delamer during
the late war. They didn't entirely understand why a good
man would shed a proud name, but they took him to have
his reasons. More than a few men riding the Brazos changed
their moniker from season to season.

"Who'll get us started at fifty?" Walin called.

"Done!" Cummings yelled.

A red-haired cowboy draped an arm over the corral rope
and bid fifty-five.

"Sixty-five!" Cummings countered.

"Seventy," the redhead replied.

"Eighty," a newcomer offered.

"Eighty-five," Cummings shouted.

"Do I hear ninety?" Walin asked.

"Ninety," the redhead responded.

The newcomer prepared to speak, but he suddenly stopped. Wil noticed a pair of cowboys on either side of the man. Their hair was wild and red.

"I'll go ninety-five," Cummings declared. "Be a good breeder, after all."

"Not with them nags," the redhead objected. "One hundred dollars. That's a fair price for three horses. And enough for that mare."

"Isaac?" Walin asked.

Cummings started to speak, but someone brushed his shoulder. The smith paled, and what words he might have spoken were forever muted.

"Hearing' no more bids, I'll call the black sold!" Walin said, gazing at Willie uneasily. " 'Less you want to have a word with somebody, Wil?"

"It's a fair price," Willie admitted. He stepped closer to the corral, though, and let the redhead have a good look at the Colt pistol resting on one hip.

"Bring that buckskin out next, Tom," Walin told his boy.

"No, the pinto stallion," the redhead commanded. "He's the one I want."

"You ain't runnin' this auction, Webb Scarlet!" Walin replied. "Don't think I didn't notice your brothers, either. Any more o' that, and I'll put a stop to the sale here and now."

"Don't know what you mean!" the redhead exclaimed, grinning as he waved to his brothers.

Willie frowned. He'd heard a tale or two about those Scarlets, and he guessed trouble was bound to come of them that day. Stu Walin seemed downright provoked, and the farmers, who Willie expected to sense trouble and back away, began to cluster around the Scarlet brothers, as if to blunt their scheming with superior numbers.

"You won't mind us biddin' on the buckskin, I know," Walin finally said. "Bring it out, Tom."

10

The auction resumed. Webb Scarlet appeared uninterested in the buckskin or the other two range ponies Stu Walin insisted on offering afterward. Isaac Cummings outbid a pair of farmers for the buckskin and managed top offer on the others, too.

"I ain't got all day, Walin!" Webb Scarlet yelled when Cummings led the three animals off to his unfinished livery. The cowboy slapped his hat against his knee, and Willie got a good look at the youthful face that hitherto had been concealed. Webb Scarlet was in his early twenties, slim and straight, with the clear eyes of a mountain cat. The beginnings of a mustache tickled his upper lip, giving him a sinister tinge.

"Bring out the stallion, Tom," Willie suggested. "Maybe our friend here can buy a horse and be satisfied."

"This one's a looker, all right," Walin observed. "Look at them black ears. Comanche I used to know was partial to black-eared pintos."

"Looks rough to me," Scarlet argued. "Like as not you broke him rough."

"I don't pound the heart out of a horse," Willie said, growing angry.

"You care to bid, Webb?" Willie asked.

"Not till I have a ride," Scarlet answered. "Fletcher here can't object to that."

"You're welcome to sit him," Willie said, motioning the cowboy toward the pinto. "But he doesn't leave this corral without a bill of sale."

"Callin' my brother a horse thief?" an elder Scarlet shouted.

"Terms o' the sale," Walin answered quickly. "Posted for any and all to see. Well, Webb?"

"I'll sit him," Scarlett grumbled. He slipped between the ropes and approached the pinto cautiously. Scarlet tried to throw a leg over the animal, but the horse stepped away, leaving Scarlet to fall to the ground. He rose, angrily scraping dung off his shirt.

"Want me to hold him still?" Tom Walin asked.

Scarlet's red face answered the boy, and Tom retreated. Scarlet charged the pinto, grabbing the halter Willie had provided. The redheaded cowboy quickly mounted, then ground a pair of sharp spurs into the pinto's flanks.

"Get off!" Willie shouted as the horse screamed in pain. "I won't have a horse of mine gouged."

"Well, I'm fixin' to own him myself!" Scarlet replied. "A hundred dollars! I bid a hundred dollars."

"Get off!" Willie ordered.

"A hundred's bid!" Scarlet repeated, digging the spurs in deeper.

An older man would have taken note of the fire in Willie's eyes. A wiser one would never have spurred the horse a third time. But Webb Scarlet was full of himself and blind with contempt. At least until a hand clasped his knee and wrenched him from atop the pinto. In an instant the young cowboy was face down in a pile of muck, and Willie was tearing his spurs off.

"Jim!" Webb Scarlet shouted as Willie slapped the spurs against the helpless villain. "Bob?"

Two elder Scarlets led three others toward the corral, but Wade Maddock cut them off with a well-aimed shotgun. A band of farmers disarmed the cowmen.

"No offense, friends," Maddock said, eyeing the Scarlets coldly. "Just seems to me Mr. Fletcher there's doin' the county a favor, teachin' your brother some manners."

"I'll teach him somethin'," the oldest Scarlet vowed.

"Will you now?" Willie asked, tossing the spurs aside and stepping past a whimpering Webb Scarlet. "What've you got to teach me, mister?"

Bob Scarlet stretched himself to his full six feet and shouldered his way past the farmers. He weighed two hundred forty pounds, but it was packed solid, and there was only iron menace to his appearance. Bob helped Webb up, then shoved him toward the waiting brothers.

"Now, you ready for your lesson?" Bob asked Willie.

"Try me," Willie urged, squaring his shoulders.

Bob Scarlet threw himself at Willie, and the two of them grappled a moment. Scarlet was a bear of a man, powerful and savage, and he had the upper hand for a moment. He slammed two good fists into Willie's side. The other Scarlets howled with delight, and Bob shoved Willie against the ropes and prepared to put a finish to things.

Willie hadn't spent many of the thirteen years after Appomattox running horses along the Clear Fork. He'd passed time on the Big Horn and wintered with the Sioux. A Sioux might give up half a foot in height and a hundred pounds of bulk, but he had quick feet. Willie stepped aside from Scarlet's next blow, then caught the bigger man's awkward lunge and threw him to the ground. Willie dropped both knees onto Scarlet's chest, stealing the rancher's breath. Even so, Scarlet tore at Willie's leg with feeble fingers.

"So you're goin' to teach me, are you?" Willie cried bitterly as he yanked the big man to his feet and laid a forearm across his nose. Bone crunched, and Bob Scarlet collapsed in a heap.

"You'll pay for this!" Webb shouted as Willie turned away.

"Wil!" Lewis Slocum screamed.

Willie turned in time to spy Webb take a pistol from a young farm boy.

"Try it!" Willie dared, drawing his Colt in a flash and firing a shot between Webb Scarlet's toes. "Go ahead! I haven't had anything live to shoot at since I dropped a goose last Tuesday. Well?"

"He didn't mean anything," an attractive woman in her late twenties argued as she slapped the pistol from Webb's hand. "We haven't had much good fortune, mister, and hard times make boys restless. I'm sorry we've brought on this trouble, and I beg your pardon."

"Emma, hush!" Bob scolded. "We never beg anything."

"No, but maybe we ought to," she insisted. "There's work enough without Webb gettin' himself kilt. You'd face

13

off this fellow next, and then where'd I be? A widow with three youngsters and a fourth on the way! And who to help but these no-account brothers o' yours.''

Emma Scarlet was a whirlwind, and she put her family to flight. Before leaving she managed to pay for the black mare and offer to take the pinto as well.

"I wouldn't have that stallion feel spurs," Willie answered. "And if you took him, that'd be the case."

"Likely you're right," she confessed.

As it happened, the man who'd bid on the black offered a hundred and five for the pinto. Willie sold the animal cheerfully.

"Looks like you've undid my auction," Walin declared as he handed Willie a roll of banknotes minus his commission. "Got six left. Want me to offer 'em up?"

Willie glanced at the few remaining buyers. Two shoeless farm boys gazed longingly at the ponies, but the others seemed more interested in the retiring Scarlets.

"Be another time," Willie said, wiping a trace of blood from his elbow.

"Sure," Walin agreed. "You make some miles south 'fore nightfall, hear? There's seven o' them Scarlets and a half-dozen hands to boot."

"Sure to keep me worryin' after 'em," Willie said, laughing. "I fought the whole Yank army and more tribes'n I can recall. Figure me to shy from a redheaded woodpecker named Scarlet?"

"You would if you had sense," Lewis advised, offering Willie a wet handkerchief. "Best to avoid a fight. You told me that yourself, remember?"

"You call this a fight?" Willie asked, slapping the young man on the back. "Naw, it's no more'n a skirmish. Little set-to like this only stirs the blood. Good for lettin' a man know he's alive."

"Maybe," Lewis muttered. "But not much good for keepin' him that way."

14

CHAPTER 3

Willie passed the balance of that afternoon at Walin's store, buying what supplies he figured to need in the coming weeks and swapping tales with the Walin youngsters. Tom was close to fifteen now, tall and lean like his papa. The others were stair-stepped from eight to thirteen, sandy-haired and bright with the wonderment youngsters took on when listening to Willie's tales of hunting buffalo with the Comanches or mining for gold in the Rockies.

"After all those adventures, how come you ended up back in Texas, Wil?" Tom asked.

"Wind blew me down, I suppose," Willie answered. "Good place, Texas. Hard but good."

"Nope," twelve-year-old Sam declared. "Only hard."

Mike Cobb and the Slocum brothers devoted those same hours to strolling Throckmorton's one dusty street with such females as they could pry from under a mother's watchful eye. Willie spied them from time to time, laughing and jawing away with this girl or that. If girls were hard to come by on the Clear Fork, young men with cash money were even scarcer around Throckmorton County. The Slocums seemed to do passably well. Little Mike, though, found himself hanging on the arm of a broad-shouldered gal who might have pulled her papa's plow single-handed. She was a good foot higher than Mike's nose, and it was a hoot to see him fighting to keep pace with her considerable stride.

"Yeah, but Trudy is nice, just the same," Mike announced later when Willie collected the boys for the ride south. "She knows horses, too. Her uncle's the blacksmith. Besides, she's got little brothers and a sister, too. Ain't easy bein' the oldest, you know."

The Slocums responded with arguments to the contrary. Willie laughed and mounted his horse. The boys were still quarreling as they left Throckmorton behind and turned south toward the Clear Fork and home.

Another time Willie would have ridden with a quicker gait. After all, he had cash in his pocket, and it was spring. There were still the six extra ponies, though, and his usually lighthearted companions were bickering like a pack of magpies. Even a dip in the river didn't cool them off.

"Why don't you boys ride home and torment your folks with all that jabberin'," Willie finally suggested.

"My grandpa's the same way," Lewis declared. "Comes with growin' old."

Willie threw his hat at them and set about tending his horses. A bit later Lamar scared up a broken-legged calf bawling in a ravine, and the four of them had a look.

"No brand," Lewis announced. "And no ma. Guess we have fresh meat for supper tonight."

"Guess so," Willie agreed as Lamar put an end to the calf's misery. "Anybody got a proper knife for the butcherin'?"

"Got this 'un," Mike said, pulling an enormous bowie knife from his boot. Willie took the blade and set about the bloody business of butchering the meat. The hide was spread out on a nearby willow's branches to dry properly. The meat was carried upriver to be cooked, and the carcass was abandoned to the buzzards.

"Good thing it was a small calf," Willie observed as he built a cook fire. "With nothin' but scrub wood and cow chips, it'd take us a month to roast a beef proper."

"Young beef's more tender, too," Mike pointed out.

"Maybe we ought to eat you then," Lamar said, poking his friend in the ribs. "Only we'd starve sure. Ain't meat enough on ole Mike to feed a skinny crow."

That set the boys to arguing again. Willie did his best to ignore it. On a trail drive there was too much work to allow youngsters any idle moments. That whittled down the quarrels considerably. But lately those three had too much time on their hands and few distractions. Roundup would take care of that.

An hour later the fire had burned down to coals, and Willie started grilling steaks. The aroma of the bubbling meat awakened the wranglers' appetites, and with the sun beginning its steep westward plunge, the air had taken on a crisp April chill. Mike nestled in closer to the fire, and the Slocum brothers followed suit.

"Won't be long 'fore we head the steers up to Kansas," Lewis whispered.

"No, six weeks or so," Willie declared. He would have spoken a bit more had not the noise of hooves splashing through the river upstream distracted him.

"Wil?" Lewis called in alarm.

"Watch the meat," Willie answered as he grabbed a rifle and turned to greet the uninvited guest.

Willie trotted twenty feet or so before spying a shadowy figure leading a scraggly mule up the riverbank. There was nothing very menacing about the newcomer. He was a hair over five feet tall, and when he doffed his weathered leather hat, a mop of dirty yellow hair fell across his forehead.

"You the fellow with the ponies?" he called.

"I am," Willie said, studying the limber young man walking toward him. A pair of bright blue eyes peered out from beneath the tangle of hair, and an easy grin spread across the face. Except for two thin chin whiskers, the youngster was as downy-cheeked as a newborn.

"Name's Dewey Hamer," the boy announced. "Got to

17

the auction late on account o' Ma's wagon broke down. Mr. Walin said you didn't sell all your stock.''

''Got six left,'' Willie said, steadying the youngster when he lost his balance.

''Ain't used to ridin','' Dewey explained. ''And ole Henry here ain't much of a mount. Maybe we could have a look at the horses?''

''Wouldn't hurt to wait a bit,'' Willie said. ''You look done in. We got some supper cookin'. Could you chew a steak?''

''Wrapped in leather,'' the boy said, leaning against the mule.

''Then come on, uh, I forget your name.''

''Dewey Hamer,'' the youngster repeated. ''Not hammer. Got just the one *m* in it.''

''I expect Dewey'll do for now anyway. I'm Wil Fletcher. Come meet my outfit.''

The youngster hurried along behind Willie toward the fire. The sight of the broiling steaks brought a gleam to the boy's eyes, but he stared hesitantly at the spot Lewis made for him beside the fire.

''Sit on down and warm yourself,'' Willie advised as he took charge of the mule. ''That's Lewis Slocum there turnin' the fork. His brother Lamar's at his side. Yonder half-pint's Mike Cobb.''

''I'm Dewey,'' the newcomer explained as he gripped each hand in turn. ''Ma and me've got us a farm up Esperanza way.''

''One o' them Iowans,'' Mike noted.

''Only barely,'' Dewey objected. ''Came out here when I was just two. Tell me I don't sound Texas!''

''Sort of a Yankee brand o' Texas,'' Lamar said, grinning. ''But give him a rope, a horse, and some size, and he'd pass.''

''Lots o' size,'' Lewis added. ''He makes Mike look tall.''

''Boys run to small in my family,'' Dewey said, poking a stick in the fire. ''Me, I'm fifteen and near as tall as my

18

pa ever got. If he'd been an inch shorter that reb ball would've missed him at Cassville."

For just one instant Dewey frowned. Then he regained his sunny disposition. Lewis turned the conversation toward the female population of Esperanza, and Dewey launched into the story of the town.

"We come west in '66, the whole pack o' us," Dewey explained. "Weren't many men, just grandpas and boys. Wasn't too hospitable back then. Indians burned us out three times, but we just went and started over. Had a bad spell o' cholera in '69, and the whoopin' cough took most o' the babies born in '71. My sister Emily lost her little girl. Now that the Comanches've been roped up and the buffalo hunters've lost interest, we do fine."

"Hard country to farm," Willie said, scratching his head as Lewis took the first of the simmering steaks off the fire. "Rock-hard and stone-dry."

"That's why we chose the land up by the Salt Fork," Dewey explained. "Where the creeks run. 'Cept for August we have fair water. And we've taken to runnin' some cows, too. Strays that wander in off the range."

"With brands?" Lewis asked sourly.

"Sometimes," Dewey admitted. "We don't keep those 'uns unless nobody comes to claim 'em."

"Hard to claim a beef that's been butchered," Lamar added.

"I never kilt a cow in my whole life," Dewey insisted as he shrank from the dark stares of his companions. "Look at me. Do I look like I eat cows regular?"

"Don't appear to me you eat anything," Lewis said, laughing. "But we'll feed you proper tonight. Grab a plate there and have a steak."

Dewey lowered his gaze and shook his head.

"Be an insult to turn down trail hospitality," Willie said, passing a tin plate nearly covered by a sizzling piece of meat. "Here's knife and fork. You go away hungry, and I'll have to skin you."

19

"He knows how, too," Mike added. "Used to run with the Comanches."

Dewey couldn't help grinning.

"I guess the four o' you can't eat it all," he observed.

In truth, though, Dewey might have been able to do it for himself. For a wisp of a boy, Dewey Hamer could outeat a small army.

"Been a time since we had meat at table," he explained between bites of steak. "Then it was bacon, month back, maybe."

"Don't you fish?" Mike asked.

"Been too busy with plantin' to visit the creeks," Dewey answered. "You sure you don't mind me havin' another steak?"

"Eat till you bust your britches," Willie said, laughing. "Save us saltin' what's left over. Maybe you ought to haul those ribs along home for your family."

"Oh, I . . . couldn't. . . ."

"Don't see how you could do anything else, Dewey," Lamar argued. "Pa's got thousands o' beeves, so he sure don't need meat. If there's anybody at home skinnier'n you, they wouldn't be able to keep their pants up. We'll fix you up a proper bundle in the mornin'. You'll be staying the night, won't you?"

"Can't go ridin' off alone on the Llano once the sun's set," Willie added. "I got some extra blankets. Besides, you'll want to look those horses over in the daylight. No tellin' what a man'd wind up tradin' for in the dark."

Dewey took one good look at the unfamiliar darkness beyond the river and readily agreed. Willie was glad of it, for the boys were too busy filling Dewey's head full of tall tales to bicker at each other. Later the three of them saw their guest had a good flat place to sleep, an extra blanket to fight off the night's chill, and all the company anyone could abide.

"Like havin' a pile o' big brothers," Dewey told Willie. The boy meant it, too.

20

Next morning, as the four of them forked down fry cakes, Dewey spoke a bit more.

"Ma'll faint dead away when I tell her 'bout this," he told his new friends. "To think o' such treatment from cowmen."

"She had hard dealin's with ranch folk, Dewey?" Lamar asked.

"Just lately. Miz Gunnerson had her garden trampled by cows this summer, and Rufe Jordan was whipped raw for runnin' some calves off his cornfield. Couple o' men rode through our fresh-plowed fields. Took a shot at me when I told 'em to stay clear."

"Know who it was?" Lamar asked angrily.

"No, but I'd recognize 'em easy enough. They had the reddest hair I seen on anybody since leavin' Iowa."

Willie exchanged wary glances with his young companions. It seemed those Scarlets got around.

The solemn looks of his companions brought a sour frown to Dewey Hamer's face. The grim talk had no effect whatsoever on his appetite, though. Willie wound up mixing another bowl of batter, for there seemed to be no bottom to Dewey's stomach.

"Never knew a man to cook up anything so tasty," Dewey remarked when he cleaned his plate of the final crumbs. "My Uncle Rupert cooked for me once when Ma was off tendin' Miz Henderson, her expectin' a baby and all. I do believe Uncle Rupe could burn bacon so you'd swear it was tree bark!"

"You take to the trail, you get so you can fend for yourself," Lamar said, imitating Willie's oft-repeated maxim.

"One thing else you learn is the cook never scrubs the plates," Willie added, turning that chore over to the Slocums. "Mike, you see to the horses. Dewey, let's have ourselves a glance at the sellin' stock."

"Sure," the boy said, bounding to his feet. "Lead away, Mr. Fletcher."

As Willie showed Dewey Hamer the six remaining range

21

ponies, one thing became clear. The boy knew the difference between the head and tail of a horse and little more.

"Truth is," Dewey admitted as Willie showed off the animals, "I only rode a mule five, six times. I can tell you my backside'd testify to that this mornin'."

"Thought it was all those fry cakes and beefsteak slowed you down," Willie said, grinning.

"Guess I'd make a poor cowboy. But I hold a plow steady. Ask around."

"I'd guess you to be doin' more'n fair for a boy who's had to grow himself up without a papa around."

"Had uncles and such. Anyway, I come to buy these horses if you'll sell 'em. Mr. Walin said they were prime stock, and you'd ask top price for 'em."

"I've always taken pride in how I work a range pony into a saddle mount."

"Mr. Walin also said you got a generous nature."

"I wouldn't ask those boys up at the camp about that. They'd likely argue otherwise."

"No, I was talkin' to Lewis down by the river this mornin', and he said you'd likely help us if you could."

"And how much is this help apt to cost me?"

"Mr. Walin said I should put the deal right out on the table, so here goes. I got a hundred and fifty dollars cash. It's every stray cent in Esperanza, I'll bet. I was hopin' to buy the six horses at twenty-five a head. We got a couple o' mustangs last year in Albany for twenty-five."

"You bought swaybacked nags in Albany," Willie muttered. "Twenty-five? I sold some half-broke Indian ponies to the army a few years back and got thirty. These are good horses, Dewey. Anybody else I'd want fifty-five, sixty."

"I know," the boy said, hanging his head. "Mr. Walin . . ."

"That's another thing," Willie declared. "If Stu Walin's so all-fired generous with my time and money, maybe he'd make up the difference in price."

"Couldn't ask him to, Mr. Fletcher. Shoot, he's already

22

carryin' us on his books for seed money. If we'd got a decent harvest last year, we'd have enough to offer you more. But you remember how dry it got in August, and mostly the corn plants shriveled up and died.''

''August out here's always dry. A man's a fool to farm here in the first place. It's buffalo country. Now they're gone, sheep and cattle try to scratch out a life.''

''We're here,'' Dewey said with solemn eyes. ''So I guess we're bound to scratch out a life, too.''

''Like as not to die tryin','' Willie grumbled.

''Some already have. A lot more will if we don't have horses to pull plows.''

''These aren't oxen, Dewey. They ain't used to harness.''

''They'll do, though. They have to.''

Dewey planted his feet and glued a hand on each hip. The boy's jaw jutted forward, and he stubbornly held out the promised cash.

''They send you out here, a scruffy boy with no pa, to play on my soft heart?'' Willie asked. ''Make me see the hard times in your eyes?''

''I heard some about you, sir. I guess maybe you known some hard times yourself. If my pa'd been the one to ride back from the war, I hope he'd find a chance to help out your people if they were in a fix. Might be he would've, too, 'cause he was the sort to hear Ma talk.''

''I could offer you three,'' Willie suggested.

''I know that's fair,'' Dewey admitted. ''But it won't do. We need the six of 'em. If you'd agree to it, I'd sign a note for the rest. I could work it off for you come winter. Or until you figured we were square.''

''I never knew a farmer who needed more debts,'' Willie said, reading the terrible despair flooding Dewey's face. ''Your pa didn't die wearin' blue so his son could be a slave.''

''We need those horses, Mr. Fletcher.''

''I suppose you do, too, to swap yourself for 'em,'' Willie said, scratching his chin. ''Tell you what. The stallions've

23

been plenty friendly with that little buckskin mare. She's the best o' the bunch. You take that 'un for yourself, Dewey. And when she pops her first colt, he's mine. That'll square us.''

Dewey handed over the money, and Willie set to writing out a bill of sale. The boy glanced at the paper in alarm, though.

"You didn't say anything here about the colt," Dewey pointed out. "Best we spell it out. Somethin' could happen, and . . ."

"What could happen that'd change our bargain?" Willie asked.

"I could catch the cholera. Or you could get run down in a stampede."

"I get trampled, I won't have much need of a colt. And if you go and die, I'll be too mad at you to take a horse off o' your ma."

A flicker of a smile came to Dewey's face. He reached over and gripped Willie's hand. There was iron in those small, bony fingers, and Willie judged himself wrong about Dewey Hamer. They hadn't sent him because he was rail-thin and hollow-cheeked. He was the kind to get a thing done.

"I got a roundup to help commence," Willie said as they turned toward the camp. "Then it's north to Kansas. Later on, though, you might like to climb atop that buckskin mare and join us in a bit o' huntin'. Who knows? We might even find a buff or two."

"I shot a deer last September up above the Salt Fork," Dewey explained. "Some good sports there. Maybe I'd show you where."

"Maybe," Willie agreed. "I'm partial to venison."

"Ma says I'm partial to anything that don't eat me first," Dewey said, laughing as he quickened his step to keep pace with Willie's long strides.

She ain't far wrong, either, Willie thought as he gazed back at the skinny youngster. But then mamas rarely were.

CHAPTER 4

While delivering the range ponies to Mrs. Miranda Hamer's little farm south of the Salt Fork, Willie had his first good look at Esperanza. Calling the place a town would have been a stretch. Really there was just a store operated by Dewey's Uncle Rupert and a long narrow building that served as town hall, Sunday meetinghouse, occasional school, an even a jail when the need arose. Otherwise the farmhouses ran along four dusty market roads that spread out like spokes of a wheel—one each headed north, south, east, and west. Cornfields and peach orchards shared the banks of a half-dozen creeks, and every farm had its own substantial garden.

"We got big plans for our town," Dewey declared as he led the way past the store. "Just north's the only good crossin' of the Dodge City cattle trail. We pooled our money and bought up the acreage. This year we'll charge a grazin' fee for cowmen to rest their herds there—or a toll to cross. Ain't figured out which yet, but either way, we'll be comin' into midsummer cash."

"Won't everybody take well to that," Willie warned.

"Oh, we thought on that. Raised a sort of citizen's mi-

25

litia, and we've advertised for a town marshal. Offered good money and a slice of that grazin' land.''

"No one man's goin' up against a trail crew, Dewey. Not but once anyhow.''

"Militia'd be there to back him up. I'm a corporal in it myself. We need the money to grow, Miz Gunnerson says. Ain't just a marshal we want. We need a doctor and a teacher. Preacher, too. Know how far we have to go to get married or proper baptized?''

"That's a worry for you, is it?'' Willie asked. "Plan on marryin' anybody particular?''

"Sooner or later,'' the boy said, hiding his face a moment. "Most likely later. Uncle Rupe says I ought to wait until I can see a gal's chin 'fore I ask her.''

Willie shared the boy's laughter. Then Dewey pointed to a small house surrounded by white pickets.

"That's it,'' the youngster added. "We built a rope corral around the side. That'll do, won't it?''

"Long as you have fair weather,'' Willie answered. "But these horses still got a tinge o' the wild in 'em. I'd build a proper corral 'fore long, and I'd hobble 'em meanwhile.''

"Sure,'' Dewey agreed. He then rode over to the rope corral, dismounted, and opened the gate. Willie then drove the six ponies inside. As Dewey closed the gate, a petite woman in her early forties emerged from the house.

"Gracious, Dewey, you've done it,'' Miranda Hamer said as she hurried over beside her son. "Rupert said you have a talent for tradin', but I never expected . . .''

"Had to make some promises,'' Dewey said, wrapping a thin arm around his mother, "but I figure it's mostly Mr. Fletcher here feelin' sorry for a horseless farm boy. Told you it ain't proper a near-growed boy should ride a mule.''

"I thank you for the generosity, Mr. Fletcher,'' Mrs. Hamer said, bowing slightly. "Won't you come in and rest a moment? I have some coffee on the boil. Perhaps you'd share our supper with us.''

"Might as well,'' Dewey added. "It's your beef we'll be

eatin'. We got a pile o' greens and bottled peaches, too.''

"Never could resist a peach, bottled or otherwise," Willie said, sliding off his horse.

"We'll save you back a bushel come pickin' time," Mrs. Hamer announced. "Come along inside. Dewey can show you the washbasin. Be nice cookin' for company. Now what's this about beef, Dewey?"

"Just let me show you," Dewey cried, untying the ropes that strapped down the rawhide bundle behind his saddle. "We'll be eatin' like kings for a week."

"More likely a month," Mrs. Hamer remarked as she gazed at the considerable package Dewey heaved onto his shoulder. "Best I make that two bushels, Mr. Fletcher."

"Please, ma'am, it's just Wil," Willie explained.

"Then you best call me Miranda," she explained. "There. It does make for easier conversation, doesn't it?"

"Yes, ma'am," Willie agreed.

Over a steaming cup of the finest coffee Willie had tasted in half a decade, Miranda Hamer repeated Dewey's tale of Esperanza and the hard times that had greeted the settlers there. It was later, after she served up beef slices surrounded by stewed carrots and tender green beans, that she spoke of the town's future.

"You know, ma'am," Willie again warned, "there'll be plenty of folks who resent a toll on the Salt Fork crossin'. Some'll consider it a hindrance. Others'll just run right through. At best it'll cause bad blood."

"And at worst?" Miranda asked.

"Bloodshed," Willie replied. "It's happened elsewhere. Out this way the range is just openin' up for cattle. But where there's a dollar to be made, a man'll happen along to make it. You run across new outfits all the time. We got three or four joinin' us for roundup. Some don't own an acre o' land, but they got a brand to stick on their cows, and if we watch 'em, they don't steal much . . . or often."

"Yeah, we had a visit or two from 'em," Dewey noted.

"It's those men who've troubled us most," his mother

27

agreed. "They run their animals across our fields, tramplin' the corn."

"Say they got a right to the water," Dewey grumbled. "But they got no title to the creek beds. They belong to us."

"Wasn't always that way," Willie tried to explain. "Back in the old days . . ."

"The lawless days," Miranda interrupted. "Won't stay that way forever. We'll soon have a proper sheriff."

"Won't change a man's thinkin'," Willie argued. "There's trouble comin'."

"Yes, I'm afraid you're right," she said, sighing. "I worry about it some, too. But storms will come, won't they? We've weathered the worst of them."

"Yes, ma'am," Willie said politely. But inside he wanted to scream out another warning. Those farmers, with their whitewashed pine houses and neat picket fences, had no notion of what a true storm was. Let them bring on a range war. Then they'd find out!

With spring roundup and a cattle drive in the offing, Willie had little time to devote to thoughts of the Hamers or Esperanza in the days to come. While Ted Slocum took charge of the western range crew and Travis Cobb directed the outfit sweeping the south and east, Willie found himself riding off with Lewis and Lamar Slocum north of the Clear Fork. A pair of TS hands, Jeremiah Dobbins and Felix Perez, followed. They were joined that night by Albert Henley, owner of the Diamond H spread, and Bart Peters, whose little Bar P place squeezed itself between the TS's northern acreage and the Diamond H. Cable Finch, who ran fifty head or so on his Songbird Ranch downriver, appeared in time for breakfast.

Roundup had never been much fun, but in the old days, when it was just a matter of running in strays and combing the range for mavericks, Willie hadn't half-minded it. Nobody much enjoyed branding the yearlings, much less the half-wild mavs. And he never had managed to hold his stomach down when it came time to geld the bull calves.

"Unsettles a man, don't it?" Travis used to quip as he went about the cutting as casually as if he were whittling.

Lewis and Lamar had tended that chore last year, and they were certain to do so again.

"I did all right after the first couple," Lewis remarked as they drove a handful of strays out of a ravine. "Then Davey Howard had to go and fry up a mess of 'em for supper. Called 'em Brazos sausages. I ate three 'fore I figured out the truth of it. Spent all night off in the brush heavin' up my supper!"

"I thought they was sort o' tasty," Lamar said, laughing at his younger brother.

"Didn't see the major helpin' himself to any," Lewis said sourly. "Pa said 'fore they started trailin' animals to Kansas, wasn't the need to do all that."

"Wasn't a market for beef, either," Willie pointed out. "We used to lose a lot of young bulls to fightin', too. Now we mostly do it to strengthen the breed. You save back most of the young cows and a tenth of the bull calves for breed-in'. Mostly you trail steers. Easier to handle on the trail, and you still have a good calf crop next year."

"Sure, I know all that," Lewis admitted. "But I'll be glad just the same when I'm old like you, Major, and can leave the cuttin' to some poor kid."

"Old?" Willie asked, swatting Lewis with a hat. "I'll show you old."

"Just joshin', Major," Lewis cried as Willie drew out a rope's end.

"Sign o' wisdom," Willie observed, and the others laughed.

Laughter and tale-swapping offered only brief distrac-tions from the task at hand, though. With four ranches sharing the north bank of the Clear Fork and cattle sure to roam where they chose, the challenge often came when deciding just which outfit owned a particular yearling. If a

29

calf trailed its mama, a cowboy hopped down and notched the youngster's ears according to the mother's brand. If a calf plodded along alone, it was marked according to the next branded animal that appeared. The same went for the odd maverick that was swept up in the roundup. The stock were officially branded once they'd all been collected.

Mostly it went tolerably well. The four brands were different enough to tell apart even when the iron hadn't made its mark any too clearly. In some places roundups had given way to outright war. More than one cowboy rested in his grave over a disputed calf. The only trouble the north-range crew had was resentment over Cable Finch.

"Why don't you buy yourself some grass instead o' eatin' mine, Cabe?" Henley eventually asked.

"Ain't there enough grass to feed anything hungry for it?" Finch retorted. "I ain't got money to throw away on lawyers and titles. I been runnin' cows here since I could spit, and I never needed title."

"You will," Willie cautioned. "Too many outfits are crowdin' in, and holdin' title's the only way to keep the newcomers off the range."

"And from stealin' our beeves," Henley added. "Enough o' that goin' on now."

"Oh?" Willie asked. "Where?"

"In front o' your nose," Peters declared. "Can't be just me's figured we've come up shy this year. No Comanches hereabouts to blame. I'd guess it's been white men."

"We'll have a look once the brandin's finished," Willie promised.

"We do, and we'll all of us take a loss," Henley replied. "We all know where the stock's sure to be, don't we?"

Peters and Finch nodded, and Willie turned to the Slocum boys.

"They're right, Major," Lamar said, scratching his chin. "I seen a rider up that way yesterday mornin'."

"Rustlers?" Willie asked.

"Of a sort," Henley answered. "New neighbors. Come

out here with nothin' but a pair o' swaybacked mules. Got 'emselves good horses and a regular house now.''

"And five hundred head or so," Peters added. "Mixed brands. I'll bet you don't find any bills of sale, either. Last year it was mostly calves. Now they got steers ready for market. And we all know whose brands ought to be on their rumps."

"On them or their cows?" Jeremiah Dobbins asked.

"Both," Henley answered.

"You must be pretty sure," Willie said, scowling. "Does Ted know? Trav? How come you two let it go without doin' anything?"

"Bart and I rode out to have words on it," Henley explained.

"Near got my ears shot off," Peters complained. "I can spare a few head easier'n my hide."

"You should've spoke up," Willie told them. "Ain't smart lettin' wolves settle in alongside the henhouse. It'll come to a fight sooner or later. Always does. Best to have it out 'fore they grow fat on your stock."

"Easy for a man without a wife and kids to talk that way," Henley growled. "You know the work, too, from what I hear. I never shot anything bigger'n a deer. And I never hunted anything that was sure to shoot back."

"Major has," Lewis countered. "Me and Lamar, too."

"Get yourselves kilt," Henley muttered.

"Ain't lookin' for a war," Willie insisted. "But you deal with thieves. We'll turn to it tomorrow."

Good to his word, Willie saddled his tall gray horse shortly after dawn and prepared to ride northward.

"Here," Lewis said, passing over a flour sack before tossing a saddle blanket over his pinto's back. "We're bound to be gone most of the day."

"We?" Willie asked. "This is a job for one man."

"Ah, Major, you can't ride off and leave us with the work," Lamar complained as he joined them. "Best Felix

31

comes, too. He knows this stretch better'n any of us. He's handy with a rifle, too.''

"There'll be no shootin'," Willie ordered.

"You don't know them Scarlets," Lewis remarked.

"Scarlets?" Willie asked. "They the ones back of it?"

"Thought you knew that much," Lamar said, frowning. "We heard a hundred stories about 'em in Throckmorton, and we didn't get into any tangles with 'em. Then when ole Dewey was here . . .''

"I figured them to be twenty miles north o' here," Willie explained. "You mean . . .''

"They got a house up that way, but to hear folks talk they ride around and scare up anything with four legs and no brand 'tween here and Mexico," Lewis advised. "There's been men ride out to talk with 'em's not come back. Others did return—with backs whipped raw. So you see, it's better there's four of us.''

"Or five," Albert Henley added.

"Forgettin' what you said yesterday?" Willie asked.

"I'm a fool, I know," Henley said, shaking his head. "But Bart and me tossed a coin. I go, and he sees I get proper buried if I don't come back.''

"Won't come to that," Willie told them. "And five men are too many. I agree to take one.''

"I got myself saddled up," Lewis announced.

"All right," Willie told the young man. "Stay in my shadow, Lewis. You others get along with the work for now. We may need you in a bit.''

"Likely you will," Henley replied. "Be cleanin' my rifle, Major.''

Willie nodded grimly, then climbed atop the gray. Lewis mounted up as well. The two of them headed off into the broken hills north of the Clear Fork. They rode slowly, quietly, with nary a word passing between them. It was time for caution, and their eyes scanned the country ahead and behind, to the right and then the left.

They wove their way ten miles through dry creek beds

and over rocky hillsides before spying so much as a single longhorn. Willie wasn't surprised. They'd done a fair job at roundup. But as they topped a slight rise, he suddenly was struck by an overpowering odor.

"Dung," Lewis whispered as he turned his nose away from the wind. "Worse'n a Kansas stockyard."

It was the truth. Moments later Willie saw why. Two hundred head were squeezed into a narrow ravine below. Three slight-shouldered boys stood a guard of sorts nearby. Their flaming red hair marked them as Scarlets.

"That's Walt on the left," Lewis whispered. "Eighteen maybe. Beside him's Randy. Sixteen, I think. That youngest one's Thad. He's not such a bad sort. I tossed some horseshoes with him once in Esperanza when his brothers weren't around. He'd kill you, though, if it came down to it. Elsewise his brother'd take a whip to him."

Willie dismounted and prepared to start down toward the ravine. Lewis began to do likewise, but Willie shook his head.

"Stay here, Lewis. I'm goin' to check the brands. I wave to you, you head back and get your papa. Twenty, thirty men. We make a big enough show, we might not have to do any killin'."

"And if they see you?" Lewis asked, pointing to the Scarlet boys.

"Then you ride even harder 'cause I'm apt to need help a hair sooner."

Lewis shuddered, but he didn't shrink from his duty. Willie flashed a smile, then stepped around a boulder and crept stealthily toward the entrance of the ravine. He reached it undetected and wasted no time crawling along the rocky slope above the cattle, searching for recognizable brands. Another man might have walked among the animals. Willie'd seen men trampled and others gored by that mass of horns and hooves. He had a fair measure of respect for the average longhorn as a result.

It didn't take long to discover a TS brand here, a Diamond H or Bar P there. Only rarely did he see the four-letter SCAR brand. And then it seemed to cover another.

Willie turned toward the hill. Lewis had hidden well. Except for a hint of buckskin, the boy was close to invisible. Willie waved, then continued. He planned to count the stock while he waited for the TS hands to appear.

"Fool," he muttered under his breath. He'd left the flour sack tied to the black's saddle horn. A cold biscuit would have tasted fair just then.

Ted Slocum was three hours getting a crew rounded up and another half hour crossing the Clear Fork and reaching the stolen cattle. By that time Willie had made his count and crawled back to his horse. The stench of the penned-up cattle and his hunger had driven him up the hill.

Lewis and his father appeared first, having ridden ahead of the main body.

"What now?" Ted asked as he scanned the ravine.

"Best speak a word or two," Willie advised. "But first put some men around to their back and some on each end of the ravine."

"Once you'd have just ridden 'em down," Ted declared as he sent Lewis to instruct the others.

"I hope I'd never run down a pair o' boys," Willie answered. "It's their brother's to blame. And once blood's shed, won't be any truce made."

"No, I suppose not."

When the others were in place, Ted Slocum stepped out and hollered at the Scarlet boys.

"Leave them rifles be!" Ted warned. "I got company."

Some of the hands fired off their guns, and the young Scarlets exchanged uneasy looks.

The shot brought Webb Scarlet galloping toward his brothers. The twenty-one-year-old drew a Sharps carbine from its sling, but a warning shot from the hill splintered the rifle's stock, and Webb reined in his horse.

"You Scarlets seem to've collected some stock that

doesn't belong to you," Ted observed. "We'll be takin' these animals back home."

"You just think you will!" Webb barked. "I got help comin'."

"This much help?" Ted said, waving his hat in the air. Twenty-four men stepped out from their hiding places. Webb paled, then glanced at his badly shaken brothers.

"We'll be goin' now," Ted added. "Be advised you don't belong on my range."

"Your range?" Webb howled. "You don't own all Texas, Slocum!"

"I own this much of it," Ted answered angrily. "And most of these cows, too. You and your brothers ride south and visit here again, throw ropes over my stock, you'll have need of spades."

"Yeah? Aim to go to war, do you, Slocum?"

"I've got right on my side," Ted declared.

"Right?" Webb screamed. "You got words on some Yankee judge's paper. I've got sweat and blood testifyin' for me. No court's hearin' any claim in Throckmorton County for a long, long time. By then I'll have the money to buy its favors. Ain't no law here, old man. You hold what you're strong enough to hold, and you don't bother those you can't beat."

"This ain't some poor farmer you can whip with a rawhide strap," Willie shouted. "We've met once, and I don't recall you gettin' the better of it. Care to try again?"

"Maybe this time we'll try pistols," Webb said, tossing his ruined carbine aside and reaching for a Colt. Willie drew first and prepared to fire the second Webb's pistol leveled itself.

"Lord, he's quick," Thad mumbled.

"Well?" Willie called. "Either toss that gun aside or try your luck. I could miss. I have . . . once or twice since the war."

"I believe you," Webb said, dropping the gun. "We'll move off now."

35

"See you don't come back!" Ted warned.

"This ain't over!" Webb yelled.

"Better be!" Ted shouted back. "You boys had all the charity and good fortune you'll find on the Clear Fork. Next time I'll be killin' somebody."

Webb turned and glared. It wasn't just anger Willie read on the redhead's face, though. Fear was there as well. He was glad. Sometimes fear turned a man cautious—wise, even.

CHAPTER 5

The final week of the roundup Willie posted a night guard around the northern trail camp. He didn't figure the Scarlets were stupid enough to challenge a big outfit like the TS, but he'd learned that a bit of caution often kept the burying spades stowed away.

That proved to be the case this time anyway. Finally the cattle were collected off the range and the branding and gelding done. Two thousand animals, mostly steers, were picked out for the trail herd, and the rest of the stock was driven off to good grass and plentiful water. Henley, Peters, and Finch managed a hundred animals between them, and a couple of ranchers south of the TS brought in three hundred more. Adding in Travis Cobb's seven hundred Circle C steers, it made close to three thousand.

"That's enough to break any crew's back," Ted Slocum announced as he studied the motley collection of cowhands and drifters that would make up the outfit. "Pray for good weather and low rivers, Major. And make your dispositions."

Willie couldn't help laughing. Ted sounded more like a general than the burly corporal who'd thundered across a dozen Virginia battlefields behind Major Willie Delamer and Captain Travis Cobb. All that seemed a lifetime ago, lost in a decade and a half of dust and blood. Those memories seldom returned now, even in nightmares. No, for once peace seemed at hand, or at least as close a version of it as was possible on the Llano.

"I figure you to run things, Ted," Willie finally replied. "If Trav takes the lead, I'll take the right flank. Give Dobbins the left. He seems steady, and he's got the best cuttin' horse in Texas."

"Who you want on the tail end?" Ted asked.

"Somebody who doesn't mind dust and youngsters," Willie said, laughing. "I'd judge Lamar ready."

"You were younger when you rode down them Yank supply wagons out of Harper's Ferry. I'll tell him what you said. He might slack off a hair for me, but he wouldn't let *you* down."

"I don't expect him to."

The other riders were meted out as needed to keep the herd headed north. That meant a few men up front on the point, with most cutting off strays and laggards on the flanks and rear. Moving longhorns a hundred feet, much less several hundred miles of broken near-parched country, was nightmare work at its best. At worst it became downright deadly.

Before heading north the crew gathered at the Clear Fork for a proper send-off. Those with wives and children said their good-byes, and those without passed time with the two wagons full of girls who'd come up from Fort Griffin to provide a jug of spirits and some amusement—and to put a few greenbacks away against the slow summer months. There were also a dozen or so girls down from Esperanza. They came mainly to share in the feast and dance a bit. The younger, wide-eyed cowboys like Mike Cobb and Lewis Slocum escorted them around like royalty, and it was enough to break a man's heart watching the shy youngsters stumble around saying farewell.

"Give me an Abilene fancy gal any day," Coley Maxson

told Willie with a grin. Maxson was cold-eyed and rock-hard from many nights on the Llano and a bit bowlegged from riding too far and too often. His grizzled stare could chill marrow. He'd turned twenty-five the week before.

"You could be right," Willie answered as he studied Trav Cobb strolling the river with Irene and the little ones. "But I sometimes wish I was ridin' off leavin' somebody worth rememberin' behind."

"Oh? Well you haven't met Delores then, have you?" Maxson asked. "Come let me introduce you."

"No, I traveled that trail before," Willie muttered. "Just makes the next day that much emptier."

"Suppose it does. Still, a man's bound to do his part to support orphans and widows."

Maxson set off toward the little city of tents that had sprung up behind the two parked wagons, and Willie walked over and cut himself a slice of bubbling brisket. He managed a nod for little Arthur Cobb, and he tossed horseshoes with Lewis and Lamar a time or two.

"Figure it to be a hard drive, Major?" Lewis asked after plunking down a third straight ringer.

"Didn't know there to be any other kind," Willie responded as he tossed a shoe half a foot short of the mark. "Life wasn't made for bare feet and soft hands."

"No, sir, it wasn't," Lewis agreed. "Not on the Llano, and sure not in Kansas."

They left just short of dawn that next morning. The first day was always a trial, what with getting the men used to each other and the cattle accustomed to rumbling northward. Some outfits managed ten to fifteen miles a day once a drive got rolling. Most made only three or four in the early going. The TS herd thundered seven before Willie called a halt. The second day they passed Throckmorton, and the third they made camp on the south bank of the Salt Fork of the Brazos.

"Guess after tomorrow we're really on the trail,"

39

Lewis remarked when he spread his blankets between Willie and Mike Cobb that night. "Leavin' the Brazos and all."

"Sure," Willie agreed as he wiped his dusty face with a damp rag. "Brazos's been home. She's a torment and a worry most times, but I do miss her salty, rock-cussed self when I'm away."

"Maybe we'll have time for a swim 'fore we leave," Mike said as he kicked off his boots and slipped his suspenders off his bony shoulders.

"Got cattle to move, son," Travis called from the fire. "Only swim you'll take's alongside the longhorns if your horse tosses you in the river."

"Don't laugh," Lewis warned as Mike chuckled. "Happened to me last time out. You get a horn up your rump, you'll know what trailin' cattle's all about."

Lewis was about to launch into a tale when the sound of approaching hooves hushed him. Instinctively Willie slid his right hand over the wooden grip of his Colt.

"Night guard don't change for three hours," Travis observed as he picked up a Winchester.

"No," Willie said, stepping toward two shadows approaching from the east. As they neared the fire, Willie breathed a sigh of relief. In rode Dewey Hamer and a fat-faced farmer.

"That's Penelope Muehlenbach's papa," Lewis said, hurriedly scrambling into his discarded britches.

"And Dewey," Mike added.

Willie greeted them with a friendly wave, and Travis poured out coffee for the visitors.

"Ain't just to be social we come," Dewey explained as he dismounted. "We come to collect the toll for the crossin'."

"You come to do what?" Coley Maxson cried, rising from his place at the fire. "Toll? Boy, this ain't Yankee country like Kansas. Here Texas cattle go where they've a mind to travel."

40

"It's always been open range here," Travis added.

"We bought title," Muehlenbach explained as he eyed the cattlemen warily. "Is our land now. Legal."

"What sort o' hog snot's this!" Maxson barked. "Chargin' to cross the Salt Fork? Next thing they'll ask a silver dollar for you to visit their outhouse."

"There's a dollar saved by you, Coley," Travis said, laughing. "You never visited an outhouse that I can recall. A few other sorts o' houses, but . . ."

"State your terms," Willie suggested as he helped Dewey down. "We don't practice lawbreaking if we can help it."

"We done a fair bit of talkin'," Dewey explained. "Ten cents a head's what we settled on, with double that if you rest the herd here and eat our grass."

"Ten cents, huh?" Travis said, shifting his feet. "You know we're leavin' behind enough manure to sweeten your crops till doomsday. Up north there's farmers glad for our passin'."

"Sure," Dewey said. "But it's our land, and we are entitled to charge. You could cross elsewhere."

"Not without losin' time," Willie noted. "I spoke some on this before, Dewey. There'll be folks ride on through and never give you a second thought. And some who'll shoot bullets at you."

"But not you," Dewey said confidently. "Ain't any of us forgot about them ponies, Mr. Fletcher. I figured you to let 'em go too cheap by half. A man's due a return on such kindness. Council said for you the toll's cut to thirty cents a head."

"Who does the countin'?" Travis asked.

"We do," Muehlenbach answered.

"No, we trust you not to cheat us," Dewey declared.

"Lewis, go fetch your papa," Willie instructed. "Ted has the say where money's concerned. We started north with three thousand beeves. That's nine hundred dollars by my reckonin'. Not a bad cash crop."

41

"No, it'll pay off some of what we owe the banks," Dewey admitted.

Willie motioned to Muehlenbach, and the heavyset farmer finally dismounted. The visitors took the offered coffee and sat with Travis on the far side of the fire. A few minutes later Lewis reappeared with his father.

"Lewis told me," Ted said to Willie. "Figure we should pay?"

"You say you have title?" Travis asked.

Muehlenbach took out a series of papers from his pocket and passed them to Travis. After looking them over, he passed them to Ted Slocum.

"Owns it all right," Ted grumbled. "We can manage your nine hundred. I'd offer this advice, though. Scale down your askin' price. Most o' them South Texas herds won't have cash money for such as this."

"Then we'll take cattle in trade," Muehlenbach replied.

"At Weatherford prices? Twelve dollars?" Ted asked. The big farmer nodded, and Ted spit in the fire. "A South Texas steer's come halfway to Dodge City now. Beeves bring twenty-five, thirty dollars at market in a low year. You'd be tellin' him he's crossed all this country for nothin'. He'd fight you rather'n admit that. And most of them South Texas bands got an outlaw or two along to keep the bandits away. Five cents with free grazin' would still make you money. And fewer corpses."

"He's right," Willie agreed.

Dewey turned to Muehlenbach, who studied the iron jaws of the cowboys and nodded.

"Then we won't be chargin' you nine hundred after all," Dewey announced. "A third o' fifteen would be five hundred."

"You could buy a lot of horses with four hundred dollars," Willie pointed out.

"But few friends," Dewey added. "That beef went a long ways toward curin' the melancholies hereabouts. Look at me. Don't you think I'm a hair sturdier?"

"Sure, you are," Willie readily agreed. "Do I see chin whiskers there, too?"

"If you look real hard," Dewey said, lowering his head in embarrassment. "But by the time we head off huntin' this fall, I'll likely have some a man can see without squintin' so much."

They spoke a bit longer—about the June heat and the perils of the trail. Then Ted announced it time for all to take to their blankets.

"We got cows to push north come mornin'," Ted reminded his companions. "And mornin's sure to come early."

CHAPTER 6

From his spot on the right flank, Willie watched with satisfaction as the herd surged northward. The young cowboys followed the lead of the veterans, and they managed river crossings and broken country with equal success. Once across the Big Wichita, Willie sighed for the first time. There was fair grass ahead and only the Pease River to cross before coming upon the sandy Red.

Evenings that June were surprisingly cool and clear. Sitting around a campfire, swapping tales with the youngsters or mending saddles, Willie felt a rare belonging. Not often had he known so well where he was and why. There was a purpose to his efforts, and good company at hand. All was right and fine.

It was an illusion. Up north, where the trail crossed the Pease River, they encountered another trail herd.

"Lord, would you look at that!" Travis pointed out to Willie as the two of them rode ahead to locate the best river crossing. "Those fools are trying to ford Deep Bottom. Drown half their stock and most of their cowboys."

"Maybe I'll have a word with 'em," Willie volunteered.

"Not alone, you won't," Travis said, leading the way. They weren't very far along in their mission when Willie spied the SCAR brand stamped on the rumps of the long-horns. Here and there a TS animal or a Bar P steer lumbered along as well.

"Guess we didn't find all the ravines north o' the Clear Fork," Travis observed.

"Guess not," Willie agreed. Nevertheless he continued riding. He meant to deliver his warning and perhaps afterward discuss the mixed brands in the Scarlet herd.

It was Bob Scarlet who turned and confronted them. The oldest of the brothers, Bob was a bit taller than the others and bulkier. His curly red hair was thinning, and his sour complexion and angry eyes gave him the appearance of a man older than his thirty years.

"You're Cobb," Bob declared as he slowed his horse. "So you must be Fletcher. Gave my brother Webb a hard time at Walin's. And back south. I'd judge you old enough to know better'n to tangle with a man who's got brothers."

"We didn't come here to fight," Willie objected.

"Then why come at all?" Bob asked. "You can't have anything to tell me I want to hear. Clear out!"

"You got cattle bearin' Slocum's brand," Travis pointed out.

"Strays. Likely they run off from your outfit. Ought to be more careful. Law of the trail says they belong to the finder."

"Law of the trail?" Willie asked. "That's a new one to me. Only law I understand says a branded animal belongs to the man who marked him. No other way'd be fair on open range."

"Especially when so many men feel they can round up their neighbor's stock," Travis added.

"I got a river to cross," Bob declared angrily. "Now get out o' my way."

"Plan to cross it there?" Willie asked.

"Good place," Bob replied. "Grass is good, and there's no steep slope."

"No bottom, either," Willie explained. "The Coman-ches call it Deep Bottom, but it's more'n deep. Deep's five,

45

six feet. Here the bed makes a turn, and the river's more like fifteen, twenty feet down. You'll drown your stock here. By summer's end the place is marked with cow skulls 'cause some fool's tried it.''

"The trail heads right here," Bob argued.

"Sure, it seems to. That's because the floods drain this way, and it keeps the good grass from crowdin' in along the bank like it does elsewhere. There's three good crossings. I'll show you one upstream or down. We'll be usin' the other ourselves.''

"Use what you want," Bob growled. "You're only tryin' to get ahead o' me and get to Dodge City first.''

"Your two hundred head won't hurt the price I'll get," Travis said, turning his horse away from the Scarlet herd. "Suit yourself. Drown!" Turning to Willie, he added, "Man knows it all, don't he?''

"You'll lose animals," Willie warned a final time. "And maybe men.''

"Get!" Bob yelled.

Willie flashed the fool a fiery stare and turned his big gray toward where Travis was hurrying back to the TS outfit. You couldn't tell a man without ears a thing.

While the TS crew swung west to where the Pease flattened out in a broad, shallow stretch, Willie remained on the eastern fringe, staring in dismay at the hopeless efforts of Bob Scarlet and his brothers to coax their longhorns into the Pease River. The wind had suddenly turned chill, and there was a strange feel to the air.

"I swear if he drowns any o' my cows, I'll notch his ears and run him to Kansas in their stead," Ted Slocum vowed as he joined Willie atop a low hill.

"We'll ride over tonight and insist on an accountin'," Willie promised. "Should've looked over the rest of Throckmorton County. A thief ain't likely to leave his best prize in the hands of the youngest brothers.''

"Oh, these animals were on the way north by then," Ted grumbled. "We've made fine time so far. Them Scarlets

46

wouldn't be a match for us. No, they had a week on us easy."

Willie started to reply, but the words died on his lips. Instead he rose in his saddle and looked on in horror as the reluctant longhorns floundered in the river. Those in the rear bunched dangerously, then turned around savagely and bolted in panic. The Scarlet flank riders galloped away, screaming to high heaven. The animals were safe, though. Once the longhorns were free of the treacherous river, they settled back down and began grazing.

Less fortunate was the slender cowboy fighting to keep the lead longhorns moving. His horse struggled to keep its nose out of the water, and a steer drove the sharp point of its horn into the frantic horse's side, possibly piercing a lung. With a bloody shriek, the horse took a final plunge, leaving its rider to struggle against a current of swimming, surging beeves.

"Hang on, Thad!" a second rider urged as he slapped his horse into the river. The second animal had no wish to share the fate of the first, and a splash marked Randolph Scarlet's plunge into the Pease River.

"No, Major," Ted argued as Willie started toward the river. "No!"

But Willie was already forming a loop in his rope. Taking care to avoid the temperamental longhorns, Willie threw his rope into the river beside a sputtering Randy Scarlet. The sixteen-year-old grasped the rope, and Willie managed to pull the soggy cowboy to shore. Young Thad had managed to splash his way to a half-submerged cottonwood. Shaking the rope away from Randolph, Willie threw it again. A weary Thad looped it around his waist and pulled it up under his shoulders. Willie then nudged his horse into a walk, and the boy was swept upstream fifty feet then drifted safely to the bank.

"Lord, mister, you saved our hides!" Thad cried, shivering from the damp and cold.

"Did that, all right," Randy agreed.

Willie turned toward them long enough to recover his rope. When they recognized his face, they paled.

"Why?" Randy asked, rocking on his feet. "I wouldn't've."

"Why not?" Willie asked. "Best recover your horses and get along to camp. You'll need somethin' hot in you to shake out the chill."

"My horse is dead," Thad said, fighting without success to regain his feet. The young man's left side was smeared red, and Randy hurried to his side.

"Mister, with them cows scamperin' every which way, our brothers won't even know we're in need till mornin'," Randy cried. "Maybe not then. I don't ask for my own self, but Thad's hurt."

"Help him up behind me," Willie suggested, and Randy lifted his soggy brother up onto the big gray's back. Willie assured himself the boy was in place, then promised to send someone back for the other Scarlet.

"I'll be all right," Randolph said, declining the offer.

"Unless those longhorns turn," Ted Slocum called, extending a hand down to the dismounted cowboy. "Come along up here behind me. Lord, Major, won't you ever grow any sense? Next thing I know you'll be patchin' up prairie wolves and rattlers."

"Maybe Comanches," Randy added, fighting to manage a smile.

"Comanches?" Ted asked. "Why, he used to ride with 'em! Hunted buffs hereabouts a whole summer with ole Yellow Shirt himself. And to hear him tell, ole Sittin' Bull and the Sioux's close to blood kin. You boys watch your hair. I understand Sioux got a partial fondness for red."

Willie thought to add a favorite tale, but Thad shuddered, and blood oozed out of the boy's side. Stories could wait. Now was the time to put a stitch or two in a torn hide and get some warmth rubbed back into tortured flesh.

Two miles west of Deep Bottom Travis Cobb already had the lead steers sloshing across the river. The twin supply wagons and the cook's caravan were already occupying a

48

hill above the Pease, and it was there Willie and Ted Slocum took the two bedraggled Scarlet boys.

"What we got here?" Nate Hancock, the trail cook, called as Willie rolled off his saddle and helped a faint Thad down. "Lord, Major, you gone and bloodied yourself up?"

"His blood," Willie said, motioning to Thad. "Caught a bit of horn in his side, I'd guess."

Hancock studied Thad's face a moment, then took off a dusty leather hat and scratched his cotton-white hair with long, bony, black fingers. "He ain't one o' ours," Hancock announced. "Why, I know him. He's one o' them red-headed bandits."

"It's mostly red blood he's worried about just now," Willie explained. "Trav told me before hiring you on that you were a good cook and . . ."

"Best cook you'll ever come across," Nate boasted.

"Trav also said you knew the healin' art. Worked for a doctor or some such."

"I did," the cook boasted. "Colonel Samuel Brookings, U.S. Army. While you was off runnin' 'round with your graycoat cavalry, I was patchin' up the ones you didn't shoot proper."

"Figure you can sew him up?" Willie asked, tearing Thad's blood-soaked shirt from his back.

"I'll get my sewin' kit," Nate agreed.

All this time Thad had managed to remain on his feet, but his eyes were now half-shut. Willie eased the boy onto a nearby blanket roll, and Thad blinked the mist from his eyes and looked up just as Nate returned with his kit.

"Lord, he can't be the doc!" the boy shouted, shrinking back as Nate stepped closer. "He's a . . ."

"Hush your mouth, boy," Nate urged as he took charge of the quivering fourteen-year-old. "I stitched up my share o' white boys, and they don't bleed any worse'n red or black 'uns."

"He better know what he's doin'," Randy warned as he climbed down from Ted Slocum's horse.

"You want to do it?" Willie asked, pointing to the jagged tear in Thad's side. Randy grew pale and dropped to his knees.

"Tell you what you can do, sonny," Hancock said, glancing up from his work. "Wriggle out o' them wet clothes and get yourself up against yon fire 'fore parts o' you take to fallin' off. You warm up some, come have a try at your brother. I ain't changed a white baby in twenty years, and I ain't startin' again now."

"It hurts!" Thad howled.

"Good!" Hancock declared. "You ain't lost the feel in your bones yet. Just let me finish 'fore you go movin' around, though. Might wind up stitchin' your ears to your tailbone."

"Howdy, Randy," Lewis spoke as he joined the gathering. "Take yourself a Pease River swim, did you? Major wouldn't give us the time off. You got a biscuit I can chew, Nate?"

"Got a rollin' pin to whack across your head, Lewis boy," Hancock replied. "Can't you see I got my hands full?"

"No, he only looks like half a handful to me," Lewis quipped. "Come on, Randy. I got some spare clothes put by. I'll give you the loan of a shirt till yours dries out."

"First see he gets the wet rubbed out o' him!" Hancock ordered. "Rub it out, boy! Hard. Fry him up a bit if need be."

"Lord, he must think he's Ulysses S. Grant!" Randy said, skinning out of his clothes. "Let's go, Lew, 'fore he starts sewin' on me, too."

"Wouldn't hurt," Lewis declared, laughing. "You look like a fresh-plucked chicken, you know."

"Yeah, ain't got my summer tan yet," Randy said, grinning as the life began to flow back into him. "Major, I thank you for what you did."

"Wasn't much," Willie answered. "You thank Mr. Hancock here when the time comes."

Randy froze a moment, then nodded. Willie didn't figure the Scarlets found much occasion to thank anyone and most especially a man of darker complexion.

Nate Hancock worked half an hour sewing up Thad Scarlet's side. Willie and Ted Slocum were another hour rubbing the damp out of the boy's soggy flesh. The two Scarlets passed the balance of the afternoon huddled beside the fire, sipping coffee and beef broth while their clothes dried in what remained of the late-afternoon sun.

"Wouldn't you know we'd get a cool day the first time somebody falls in a river," Willie grumbled as he checked the progress of the river crossing.

"You're the one told me life wasn't made for walkin' barefooted or some such," Lewis remarked. "Anyhow, I wouldn't worry much over them boys. To hear them talk, their brother Bob's worse'n any cold river dunkin', and they lived through a bunch o' years with him."

"Don't seem bad sorts, just the same."

"Wouldn't want to tangle with Randy in a grudge fight. He don't look like so much, but he's got meanness in him."

"The kind that'd dig spurs into a horse?" Willie asked.

"Worse. I saw him bite a chunk o' ear from Cyrus Parker a year ago last summer. No reason for such. The two of 'em was arguin' over a horsehide vest for sale at Walin's store. Anybody gone to tell Bob what's happened to his brothers?"

"Not as I know. Truth is, I think the Scarlets are too busy roundin' up their herd to notice they're shy two boys. You volunteerin'?"

"Not me," Lewis insisted. "I never go lookin' for trouble. There's enough finds you anyhow."

Willie nodded his agreement.

They continued their ride along the river, riding over to coax a reluctant steer into the river from time to time or scare a stray out of some tangle of brush. Once the animals were all on the far bank, Willie returned to camp and accepted a cup of coffee.

"How're you feelin', boys?" Willie asked the Scarlets.

"Some better," Randy said, gazing up. "Lew's shirt's a little big, but it does cover most o' me this way."

"You look in pain," Willie observed.

"He's got a bit o' black to him," Hancock explained. "On the bottom end."

"Rock bruise," Randy was quick to say. "That or bein' around Nate there's rubbin' off on me."

"What's that?" Hancock hollered. But Randy was grinning, and the cook nodded. "Couldn't help but pretty you up some, bandit."

"Maybe so," Randy mused. "Maybe so."

If Randy's spirits were revived, though, Thad was a picture of gloom. Even wrapped in three blankets, he shivered with cold.

"Fever's set in," Hancock told Willie. "Best you put him in my bed back o' the caravan. Won't hard ground do him any favors."

"You figure it's the wound or the cold, Nate?" Willie asked.

"Don't know it matters much. I dosed him some with tonic, and I gave him a good gulletful o' broth. Ain't holdin' it down, though. Don't get better, might haul him to a doc."

"You know any south of Dodge City? Nearest one I know of's in Albany."

"Doc Spanner," Hancock muttered. "Better the boy's trusted to me. I ain't got half a bottle o' whiskey sloshin' 'round in me."

Willie carried Thad Scarlet to the caravan himself. The boy seemed sturdy enough on horseback, but it was all mirage. In truth he was just a hair over five feet tall and even wrapped in blankets couldn't have weighed eighty-five pounds. The feel of the feverish boy tore at Willie, brought back the memory of others . . . in the Wilderness and at Petersburg. For the first time in ages recollections of the war haunted him.

52

"You all right, Major?" Hancock asked as he helped Willie ease Thad onto the narrow bed.

"No," Willie confessed. "Was rememberin'."

"Thought so," the cook said, drawing out a pocket flask. "Don't you tell them others I carry it. You know Mr. Slocum don't abide spirits on the trail. But sometimes the melancholy eats at an old man—one who's seen what I seen—and I need a swig. Just like you do right now."

Willie took a pull at the flask then returned it. "I'm not a drinkin' man," he explained, "but it's death that's come creepin' up on me tonight. Unsettles me some."

"Recognized it. Comes to pay me a call some nights, too. Saw how you looked at that boy. Buried one or two in your time, I'm guessin'."

"If it'd been one or two, I could stand it. And one or two would be too many."

"Sure, it would be," Hancock agreed, sipping the whiskey before passing it back to Willie. Young Thad stirred some then, and his eyes opened wide.

"Where am I?" he mumbled.

"Safe," Willie reassured the youngster. "With the TS outfit. You fell in the river and . . ."

"Got gored," Thad said, wincing. He drew back the blankets and stared at his bandaged side. "You do that?"

"He did," Willie explained, nodding to Hancock.

"Be hard times come o' this," Thad said, rubbing a tear out of his eye.

"You'll be all right," Willie said. "Randy's over at the fire. You want him to sit with you a bit?"

"Won't make it no better. Does Bob know?"

"I don't think so," Willie said, folding the blanket back over Thad's chest.

"He ain't fond o' takin' favors off strangers. And black men, well . . ."

"Don't tell him who it was," Hancock suggested.

"He'll find out. He's that way. And when he does, he'll whip the daylights out o' me'n' Randy both."

"If he's human, he'll be glad you weathered the fever," Willie argued.

"That's just it," Thad whispered. "Ain't a ounce o' human bein' to Bob nor Jack nor Webb. Walt and Randy ain't so bad, 'less they been riled, and Steve's downright good-natured. Bob's meaner'n spit, though."

Thad rolled onto his side in spite of the pain and showed off the faint white tracings left on his back by a bullwhip.

"Won't anybody whip you here," Willie vowed.

"No, he'll wait for later," Thad said, shuddering.

CHAPTER 7

Dawn brought a restoring warmth to the land. It was June once again, and the summer sun broke the horizon like a bright yellow dish.

"How's Thad?" Willie asked Nate Hancock as the cook slapped slices of ham onto plates and added pairs of fluffy biscuits.

"Fevered most the night, Major," Hancock explained. "I'll be drainin' that side once I get this outfit fed. Be two, three days 'fore he goes anywhere."

"Best somebody ride over and tell his people," Ted declared.

"That's for me to do," Randy announced. He was wearing his own mud-spattered clothes now, and his grim gaze attested to the dread he felt riding to his brothers' camp with sour news. "I'd value the loan of a horse."

"I'll fetch you one," Lewis volunteered.

"Want some company?" Willie asked.

"Wouldn't make it better," Randy explained. "I'll be back later to fetch Thad. Bob wouldn't have him left here."

"Won't do him much good to move 'round," Hancock warned. "Bad enough in my caravan. Sittin' a horse'll open him up."

"I know," Randy confessed. "But I don't have much say-so, you know. Bob'll want him with the rest of us."

They didn't argue the point. Randy rode off alone after cleaning his plate, and the TS outfit set about their duties.

Randy Scarlet returned later that morning with his brother Bob. They brought back the loan horse and another besides.

"I'll thank you to hand over my little brother," Bob growled. "You got no right holdin' onto him nor puttin' a black man to work on his wounds."

"Should've left him in the river to bleed to death, eh?" Willie countered. "You're a fool, Scarlet. If you'd had ears for my words back on Pease River, Thad never would've needed sewin' up. And now you'd sit him atop a horse so he can bleed himself white all over again."

"Whatever I do, it's my business!" Bob stormed.

"Not anymore," Willie objected. "I'm takin' a hand in it. Done all the buryin' I care to, especially where boys are concerned. You didn't pull him out of that river, and you didn't see he was mended. If you'd looked for him, or Randy either, you'd found our camp easy enough."

"I've taught my brothers to look after themselves."

"Then leave 'em to do that," Willie said, glaring. "Now, we've got some other business to settle. Should've squared accounts last night, as I promised I would, but I had other worries. We'll be visitin' your herd, siftin' out what belongs with us, and drivin' 'em north."

"You won't touch a head!" Bob shouted.

"You're the worst sort of fool," Willie said, shaking his head. "I counted five of you besides Randy here. I'd ride the whole batch of you down myself if I wanted. You can't even manage a river crossin'. You'll never see the north bank of the Washita, much less the Arkansas."

"We're new at it," Randy replied.

"What's left of your herd? A third? Sixty, seventy head, and some of them borrowed off your neighbors?"

"More like a hundred," Randy answered. "We lost half."

"Make you a bargain, Scarlet," Willie offered. "You leave Thad where he is. He'll mend proper in a day or so, and he can ride wherever he wants. Meanwhile, I'll send some men back to hurry along your beeves. And ours that're travelin' with 'em. Join the herds. For what lies ahead, a few extra men wouldn't be unwelcome, and another hundred beeves won't make for a lot more work."

"You'd take our steers?" Randy asked.

"For how much?" Bob added.

"You and your brothers'd do a share of the work. Get no wages, but there'd be no charge, either. Once we're across the Arkansas, we shake out who owns what, and each man's paid accordingly. Be no need to make a fuss over those odd brands, either," Willie whispered. "They'd just be added to their owner's list."

"Why would you do that?" Bob asked, his eyes burning with suspicion."

"Way I see it," Willie explained, "it's either this way or we kill the bunch of you."

"No stomach for a fight, eh?" Bob asked.

"Wouldn't be a fight," Willie replied. "Just some shootin'. And the buryin'. I put some time in fishin' two o' you Scarlets out o' Pease River, and it'd prove a downright waste to bury you now. If we'd wanted to shoot you, we'd done it back in that ravine. Nobody would've questioned us, seein' how you had our stock and all."

"I'd come to settle accounts."

"That might cost a few bullets. Nothin' more. Join us or bring over the borrowed beeves. Or sing a death song."

"Bob, it's a fair offer," Randy argued.

"You trust him?" the elder Scarlet asked.

"To do what he says? Yessir, I do. It was a fair risky thing he did, ridin' down to the river and throwing Thad and me a rope. And he could've kilt us easy in that ravine. Or at the river, either one. What say, Bob? Take him up on it?"

"We'll ride with you to Dodge City," Bob muttered.

"But don't get any notion this is any more'n a trail truce."

"An alliance of convenience," Willie suggested. "Nothin' more."

"Then I'll leave Thad be for the time bein' and hurry my stock along."

"I'll send 'em some help," Willie said, turning away.

"I can tend to my own business," Bob barked.

"As I can," Willie retorted. "Some o' the TS and Circle C is mixed in with your stock, remember? My five men'll just help sort all that out."

Bob Scarlet grumbled to himself as he rode off, but Randy offered a silent nod of gratitude as he returned the borrowed TS pony. Willie led the horse back to the remuda, then set off to tell Ted of his deal with the Scarlets.

"Well, that's one way to get our stock back," Ted said, shaking his head. "Major, I do believe you'd bed down in a nest o' rattlers! Scarlets and snakes, they're about the same thing. Ain't I glad to be runnin' this outfit?"

"Figure I overstepped myself?" Willie asked.

"No more'n usual," Ted said, laughing. "It's that half-dead boy you dragged in. You got a soft spot for youngsters, and it'll get you kilt one o' these days. Miracle it hasn't happened already! Grab your five hands and bring them Scarlets in. But I warn you to keep up a watch. They don't rattle 'fore they bite like some snakes."

"I'll keep that in mind," Willie promised.

Bill Delamer, Willie's father, had once taught his son the best kind of ally is an enemy turned to your side. Hadn't he, after all, made peace with Yellow Shirt's Comanches, and them the scourge of the Texas frontier? There's an understanding that comes between two proud men, and many a time Willie'd found a fight brought about a kinship he'd never otherwise discovered.

There was no such kinship between the Scarlets and the Slocum outfit. Travis Cobb never made any effort to overcome his bad feelings toward the "red bandits," as young

Mike called them. Bob and the older brothers kept strictly to themselves. Randy did fall in with Lewis now and then, and once Thad was able to ride, he rarely left Wil Delamer's shadow.

"Ain't altogether Bob's fault he's how he is," the boy said often. "He's had his hard times, you know."

"So have we all," Willie observed. "But it's rarely turned me against the whole human race. And I've never taken another man's stock for my own."

"Others have," Thad said sourly. "Wasn't so very long ago my pa had as fine a ranch as you'd find in all Texas. Then come the war, and he got kilt. Neighbors fell on our place, takin' anything not nailed to the floor. We had fifty horses. Good ones, too. Man come by and took every one, leavin' us a paper that wasn't worth a nickel once the South went down."

"You can't go and make war on everybody 'cause of that," Willie argued.

"Maybe you can't. Bob can."

Willie worried some over Thad's grim statements and the fearful way he eyed his older brothers, but soon more pressing matters came and buried those concerns.

First, the herd had a difficult time crossing the Red River. The sandy banks were a maze of quicksand even in the best of times, and crossings changed from year to year. The only way a man could be sure of his trail was to find a local guide. When one couldn't be found there was nothing to do but send a man across and trust him to have some luck. That year two horses sank in the boggy river before a crossing was mapped out. Willie deemed it good fortune no man sank as well, for Coley Maxson was waist-deep in the muck before Willie and Travis dragged him out with their ropes.

"Fool quicksand done sucked my boots off!" Coley complained when he crawled onto solid earth.

"I seen a man lose his britches that way once," Ted said, laughing as Coley hopped around, scraping orange goo from his legs.

"I got a spare pair o' pants," Coley said as he peeled off his old ones. "But boots's hard to come by!"

"I got some moccasins," Lewis said, laughing at the red-faced cowboy. "You can buy you some new boots in Dodge City. Or swap some off a Kiowa."

As it turned out, Coley did just that. Three days north of the Red River the herd was bedded down on Kiowa land, for which the tribe demanded payment of two dozen beeves.

"You boys'll make your fortune chargin' tolls," Ted told them as he had Lamar and Jeremiah Dobbins cut out the price of passage.

"Maybe so," an English-speaking chief named Lame Crow answered. "We need beef now you Texans shoot all the buffalo."

"Yeah, it's a hard road we all travel nowadays," Willie added. He then spoke a few remembered phrases learned in his Comanche days, saying he, too, missed the warrior trail. Lame Crow let loose a howl and a torrent of Kiowa, and the next thing Willie knew the chief had ordered up a full-blown celebration. There was food and dancing and tale-swapping to stir the heart. The younger Kiowas challenged the cowboys to wrestling bouts and races, and the wagering was nearly as heated as the bartering.

"A man could make his fortune if he had enough to-bacco," Coley said as he wrapped a beaded serape around his shoulders and stepped into a new pair of boots.

The cowboys fared rather poorly when it came to foot-racing, but they held their own when the grappling began. After all, a fellow used to throwing yearling longhorns around wasn't much put off by a hundred twenty pounds of Kiowa.

It was the horse races that brought out real wagering, though. No cowboy ever born wasn't proud of his horse, and the Kiowas weren't any different.

"Ain't a man in the company's got a pony can test that Kiowa boy with the buckskin," Travis observed. "But you and your gray can take him, Willie. Blindfolded, I'd bet."

"Oh, racin's for the youngsters," Willie argued. You don't see Lame Crow mountin' up."

"Then loan Mike your horse," Travis pleaded. "He's got a little wild Indian in him, I guess, 'cause he rides like a Comanche."

"I do fair," Mike admitted when Willie presented his horse to the fifteen-year-old. "But I'm not the one to do it. Hate to admit such a thing, but the best rider in the outfit's Randy Scarlet."

"What?" Willie asked. "He got himself throwed off in Pease River."

"Can happen to anybody on a horse that doesn't take to water," Mike said, throwing words Willie himself had once spoken right back in his face. "Trust him with your horse, Uncle Wil?"

"If you do, Mike," Willie answered.

"I'll fetch him then," Mike said, hurrying off. Randy returned a moment later with a smile two feet wide.

"I'll win sure enough, Major," the sixteen-year-old vowed.

"Better," Willie urged. "You don't, that Kiowa wins the bet and my horse to boot."

"Yeah, I know," Randy said, turning solemn. "You don't have to risk it."

"Pride o' the outfit's at risk, too," Willie added.

"Then I'd best win," Randy concluded as he mounted the horse and set off to challenge the Kiowa's buckskin.

The race was something to see. The Kiowa boy, Lame Crow's nephew, painted his horse with lightning bolts, and he'd stripped to nothing but a cloth breechclout. Instead of a saddle, he'd laid a blanket across the animal's back.

"Lightens the load," Willie explained to a confused Randolph Scarlet. "Don't worry. The gray's used to haulin' me."

"Wouldn't hurt to shed some weight just the same," Randy said, unlacing Willie's saddlebags and passing them down. He kicked off his boots and stripped his shirt. Then, fixing the young Kiowa with a solemn stare, Randy nudged the gray toward the starting line.

As was common to Kiowa races, the course wasn't a flat-out run. No, there were twists and turns and a pair of creeks to jump.

"Hold him steady till the end and then give him his head," Willie advised. "Ain't prairie fire can catch that horse in a straight run."

Willie thus wasn't surprised when the Kiowa took an early lead. That slip of a boy had his pony ducking beneath branches and nearly scraping boulders and tree trunks alike. Randy kept himself close, though, and the big gray wasn't even lathered when it made the final turn and prepared for the homestretch.

"Ayyyy!" the Kiowa screamed as he slapped the buckskin into a gallop.

Randy gave a cry as well, but was mostly for effect. The gray sensed it was time to run, and it let fly.

"Look at that horse go!" Travis shouted. "Winged Pegasus must've been his pa!"

The Kiowas didn't understand the comment, but they found the heart to cheer a strong horse. The buckskin's lead dropped away each second, and Randy soon surged past in a blur of hooves. The young Kiowa finished two lengths behind, seemingly lost in a cloud of tossed cowboy hats and howling Kiowas.

"Yours is a good horse," the crestfallen Kiowa remarked when he led the buckskin over and placed the reins in Randy's hands. "Mine also. Take care of him."

"Major?" Randy said, turning reluctantly toward Willie. Any fool could see the buckskin and the boy were one.

"Thank him for the good race he gave you," Willie advised. "And promise you'll care for that horse as he has."

"But I can't . . ."

"Don't insult him," Willie warned. "Let him be a man. He can ride. He'll win another horse."

"Yeah, I guess he will," Randy said, patting the buckskin's nose. "Just about had himself a big gray. I near lost my head on a blackjack oak branch near that last creek."

"You're apt to grow old then," Willie observed as he took charge of his horse again. "Learnin' to duck helps a man live longer."

After celebrating with the Kiowas another day, the TS outfit continued its journey north. There were more rivers to cross, other tribes to visit, and worse perils to face.

Up beyond the South Canadian River they had their closest call. Just short of twilight a dozen men made a charge on the right flank, firing off pistols and setting the cattle off in a westward run. While Travis Cobb moved to cut off the stampede, Willie took charge of a half-dozen men and tried to fend off the attack. There were plenty of shots exchanged, but a man flying along on horseback was a tough target to fix in one's sights, and nobody had much chance of hitting anything more than a few yards away. The rustlers closed the gap, though, and for a few minutes there was a bloody exchange at close range.

"Major, I'm hit!" Lamar Slocum cried out as a bullet shattered his left arm.

Seconds later Steve Scarlet vanished in a cloud of smoke and fire.

"Let's take 'em!" Coley Maxson urged, and Willie waved the cowboy along. The two of them charged three riders closing in on the wounded Lamar, and the rustlers turned in surprise. Willie fired twice at each of the first two men, and they slumped in the saddle. Coley killed the third. The others turned to offer some resistance, but Willie dropped another, and a band of TS hands led by Ted Slocum set the rest to flight.

"Put 'em to shame, didn't we?" Coley howled.

"Sure, we did," Willie said, staring at the sober faces of the fallen outlaws. Then he noticed Coley's lip quiver. The cowboy dropped his pistol and wavered a moment before steadying himself.

"Coley?" Willie called.

The young man grinned, then stared down at his left leg. Blood ran the length of that leg from a bloody hole in Coley's side.

"I'll help you to the cook caravan," Willie offered. "Nate can fix you up."

"Look to Lamar," Coley suggested. "They've gone and shot my back all to pieces. Can't feel my toes. Bury me deep, won't you? I got a terrible dread o' wolves."

Coley managed a final laugh before falling across the neck of his horse. He was dead before Willie got him to the wagons.

CHAPTER 8

They buried Coley Maxson in a deep trench on a hill above the river. Steve Scarlet rested in a like hole at his side. Young Steve wasn't but a year older than Randy and was well-liked by nearly everyone.

"He was a good hand," Jeremiah Dobbins said at the burying. "Slow to rile and quick to laugh. He'd've made a good cowboy by summer's end."

The TS outfit was equally sobered by Coley's passing. He wasn't possessed of so fine a character, maybe, but he'd been with Ted Slocum since turning fifteen, and ten years of swapping tales and sharing dangers melds a man to his companions.

Willie spoke little of either death. He did help Nate Hancock pry the bullet out of Lamar's arm and set the splints in place. As to letting go of emotion, well, Willie had learned to hold a tight rein on himself.

"Seems like a lonesome place to die," Thad remarked as he rode at Willie's side that night on guard. "Did you see Steve? Major, they just shot him to pieces. Wasn't any need to shoot him so many times."

"No, but I don't expect the boy felt much after the first one. As to lonely places, Coley's there, and he was always quick with a joke. They'll pass eternity in good spirits, I'd bet."

"Could've been me," Thad said. "At Pease River or yesterday. Dead and buried."

"Can't dwell much on it," Willie said, swallowing a surge of sadness. "It happens. Older you get, the more friends you leave behind."

"Wasn't just a friend," Thad pointed out. "Steve was my brother."

"I buried a brother once, too. And plenty more that were close as one. Comanches might cut 'emselves, bleed with the pain. But it's no different in the end. You ride on."

"I guess. Cattle are awful nervous tonight. Guess they know, too."

"Always that way after a stampede. I feel a storm comin' on, too. Try a song. It helps settle 'em down."

"Don't know many songs."

"Anything'll do. Steers just want the noise."

Thad started in with a marching song or two, then tried "The Yellow Rose of Texas" and "Tenting Tonight."

"Those are soldier songs," Willie noted. "Who taught 'em to you?"

"Bob. Picked 'em up in his Confederate army days."

"Don't figure him old enough to've soldiered then."

"Didn't at first," Thad explained. "Only toward the end. Pa and Uncle Red got kilt in Mississippi, so Bob went up to even the score. He's all for an eye for an eye, you know. If you hadn't dropped those rustlers, he'd've gone after 'em, squared the tally for Steve. Anyhow, when he come back from the war, we were just boys, Randy, Steve, and me. Webb, Walt, and Jim weren't much older. Wasn't much to do come nightfall, and Bob didn't know any songs but those and hymns. We Scarlets ain't much for churchgoin' or attendin' meetin'."

"Don't do it much myself," Willie confessed. "But I'm long on prayin', especially when I come to a tight spot."

"Me, too," Thad admitted. "But it ain't done me a lot o' good. Nor Steve any at all."

*   *   *

In the days that followed, there were more rivers to cross and more storms to weather. Twice more raiders stalked the herd, but the sight of thirty-five well-armed drovers kept them at bay. Only once did anyone make a move toward the herd and then it was by stealth on a moonless night. Of the six outlaws who tried, five fell to the fury of the Texans' rifles. The sixth survived long enough to be hung the next morning.

"You're a hard-hearted bunch," the outlaw claimed as Bob Scarlet slipped a noose around his neck. "There's three of my brothers dead here, and two cousins besides. My poor ma won't have anyone to look after her now."

"Guess not," Bob said as he motioned his brother Jack to raise the rope. "But I judge any mother with four thievin' sons would be happily shed of 'em just the same."

Soon afterward the TS outfit crossed the Cimarron River and left the worst of the outlaw country behind. It wasn't far to the Arkansas now—and Dodge City. Ted Slocum and Travis Cobb rode on ahead to dicker with the buyers, and Willie took charge of the day-to-day running of the crew. The men knew their business now, though, and there wasn't much to do.

"Just fatten up the beeves and dream of hot baths and fancy women," Lamar declared. "Figure they'll give a wounded hero a smile, Major?"

"Don't find any cut-rates in Dodge, boy," Jeremiah Dobbins said, laughing to himself. "Those gals'd keep company with a mountain goat if he had the price in cash money."

For the most part Willie left them to their jests and boasts. Oh, he'd sip a mug of coffee or listen to a bit of singing, but mainly he passed the evenings riding along the river, staring at the distant lights of Dodge City, and recalling other times spent there.

"I got an aunt lives not far from here," young Mike Cobb said when Willie joined the boy on night guard. "Place called Edwards."

67

"I've been there," Willie explained. "Not much of a town."

"You knew Aunt Ellen, didn't you?"

"We grew up together in Palo Pinto County. Your papa, Ellen, and me."

"Pa said we'd ride over for a visit when the cattle are sold. Maybe you could come along."

"No, it'd be family."

"Well you're just about family. I mean, I call you Uncle Wil and all. Pa says you and he's brothers of a kind. So you'd be family, all right."

"I don't know," Willie muttered, trying to shake the longing to see Ellen again.

"How come?" Mike asked. "Pa says you were real close once. Talked of getting married even."

"She married somebody else," Willie explained. "Somebody better."

"Doesn't mean she wouldn't welcome a visit," Mike argued. "She's got a boy named for you. Did you know that?"

"Yes," Willie grumbled.

"Means she ain't forgot. And you ain't."

"Oh?"

"You talk in your sleep some," Mike said, grinning. "No, you ain't forgot."

But I wish I could, Willie thought. Be better for everybody if I could.

Ted and Travis returned around midnight with news to celebrate.

"First herd in this year," Travis declared. "Got top price. Forty-five dollars!"

"Ole Trav had those buyers biddin'," Ted explained. "Chicago's hungry for Texas beef, it seems."

"Forty-five don't seem so good a price to me," Bob Scarlet remarked. "I heard people got fifty or sixty early in the season."

"Sometimes," Willie confessed. "Not this big a herd, though, and not the past few years. Too many steers makin' the trip. Top price last summer was what, thirty-eight, forty?"

"Forty-two, as I heard it," Ted said. "We settled for forty, and that was in June. I heard some o' the South Texas outfits sold out for less than twenty, and a few wound up drivin' their animals up to Nebraska or Colorado and sellin' 'em off by fives or tens."

"Sixty's a dream nowadays," Travis agreed. "Love to see it, but it's a dream."

"Well, you didn't speak for me," Bob insisted. "Tomorrow me and my brothers'll cut out our beeves and make our own deal. Fatten 'em up a week maybe."

"Be a while before they'll buy another head," Travis explained. "The pens won't hold three thousand head. We'll ship twenty-two hundred and leave the balance to wait for space in the pens. Train's due in day after tomorrow and another later in the week. You could have a long wait if herds start showin' up, and they will. I didn't pledge you'd sell, nor Henley, Peters, or Finch. It's your call, but I'd advise it."

"You got our animals," Henley spoke up, and the other two nodded their agreement.

"Not mine," Bob objected.

"We'll help you cut out your stock come daybreak," Travis offered. "And wish you luck."

"Randy, Thad, best you two come along and share our camp down by the river," Bob announced. "This is where we part company."

"I already got my blankets spread," Randy complained.

"I got friends here," Thad added.

"Get movin'!" Bob ordered, and the two younger Scarlets collected their gear and followed Bob.

"Figures we'd cheat him," Lewis observed once the Scarlets passed from view.

"No, he just can't stand to take advice," Willie grum-

69

bled. "Nor help. Cost him some money this time, but at least it didn't get a brother half-kilt."

"No, not yet anyway," Travis added.

The Scarlets soon learned the folly of their ways. While first TS and Circle C steers and later the other odd Clear Fork brands were counted by the Chicago buyers, the fifty-two SCAR beeves remained on the Arkansas, chewing peacefully, until a party from town arrived to explain the grazing fees assessed unsold herds. Bob quickly rode into town and started dickering with a pair of Kansas City buyers, but neither came close to offering forty dollars a head.

That afternoon Bob swallowed his pride and located Ted Slocum at the Lone Star Saloon.

"Is it too late to cut in on your deal?" Bob asked.

"You'd have to check with the buyers," Ted replied. "We've finished the count and been paid. There's Tobias Kirby over there at that side table. Ask him."

Bob stepped over to where Kirby and two other buyers were playing cards with a Dodge City banker. Willie didn't hear the conversation, but it wasn't hard to guess the gist of it. The buyers laughed a bit and pointed to the door.

"You should've sold," Jeremiah Dobbins called from the bar. "Captain Cobb never steered a man wrong in his life."

Bob slapped his hat against his knee and turned away angrily from the jeering cowboys.

"Man's mule-stubborn and poorer for it," Travis observed.

That night Willie was soaking a month's grit and a life-time's weariness from his hide at Ming's Bathhouse when Thad Scarlet stepped over to Willie's tub.

"Maybe you heard. We sold out for thirty-two," the youngster explained. "I just wanted you to know Randy and I don't hold with the hard words Bob's had for you and the others."

"Hard words?" Willie asked.

"Claims Mr. Slocum turned the Chicago buyers against him. They wouldn't offer a nickel. Only that Kansas City fellow made a bid."

"I could argue, Thad, but your brother'll believe what he will."

"I know," Thad admitted. "Just wanted you to know I don't share the notion. Best I get along now. You got your outfit here, and they ain't made us Scarlets any too welcome here lately."

"You boys got a grudge against Thad here?" Willie called.

"Not him," Dobbins answered. "He ain't said nothin'."

"Find yourself a tub and take a soak, Thad," Travis urged. "Place is all paid for till nine o'clock. Wouldn't hurt that side to get itself cleaned, I'll bet."

"No, sir," Thad said, managing a grin. As he stripped his shirt, though, Willie observed the jagged scar left by the horn was healing well. The dozen fresher red marks left by a lash were open sores.

"Bob's hard sometimes," Thad explained when he noticed the eyes on his back. "He's had to be."

"He's your brother, and I won't speak ill of him to you," Willie said, swallowing a growing rage. "But if you get enough of him, come run horses on the Clear Fork. I can always use the company."

"Thanks," Thad said, nodding his head solemnly. "But bad as he is, he's my brother."

"Can't let him pull you down, Thad," Willie argued. "I got a brother would've dragged me under. Shoot, he tried to have me killed. Some men are best left behind."

"Maybe," Thad admitted. "But Bob saw me raised, went hungry so I could eat. I'll stick by him."

"Sure," Travis said, frowning. "Just don't let him get you kilt, Thad. There's those o' us worked too hard mendin' you at Pease River. And 'fore you go back to your brothers' camp, drop by Nate's caravan and ask him to salve those stripes on your back."

71

"Thanks," the youngster said as he slipped into a nearby tub. "Major, maybe We'll see each other some in Dodge."

"Not likely," Travis answered. "We're off tomorrow to see my sister in Edwards. Then it's back home."

"In Texas, then," Thad said hopefully.

"I wouldn't hide if I was to see you comin'," Willie said, laughing at the shaggy redhead. "Might should if you're as dirty as you are now."

"Grit washes off," Thad said. "More'n I can say for ugly."

"He'll do, won't he?" Willie asked the others. They laughed their agreement.

CHAPTER 9

Edwards, Kansas had never been much of a place. There was the one main street leading from the railroad depot and boasting the odd assortment of buildings common to railroad towns. Beyond a pair of dusty roads led east and west from the north bank of the Arkansas. Farmhouses were sprinkled along those roads at odd intervals, and occasionally a freight wagon would roll along one or the other on its way to pick up supplies at the depot.

Edwards boasted a church and a school—even a hotel. Willie recalled the place full of life, with pranking youngsters running here and there and merchants busily pursuing their vocations. When he led Travis and Mike Cobb down Front Street, Willie couldn't help noticing the difference. Store windows were boarded up. Here and there a gap attested to some structure torn down or hauled off to a new site. The hotel had burned, and only a black scar marked its site.

"What's happened?" Mike asked, studying the deserted street.

"Don't know," Travis answered.

"Plain enough to see," Willie grumbled as he came to the stone foundation where the church had once stood. "The town's gone and died."

"Died?" Mike asked.

"Happens," Willie said sadly. "People moved on to Dodge maybe. Some anyhow," he added, noticing how the little churchyard with its stone markers and picket crosses now spread out across the hillside beyond.

"It's downright spooky," Mike observed.

"Sure is," Willie agreed. He spied a woman feeding chickens behind what used to be the mercantile, and he rode over that way. "Mornin', ma'am," he called. "I was wonderin' if Dr. Trent still lives hereabouts."

"He does, cuss his soul!" she shouted.

"The gabled house, on the edge of town?"

"If somebody hasn't gotten 'round to burnin' the place," she muttered. "Now leave me be!"

"Not exactly friendly, eh?" Travis asked.

"There's been some sort of trouble," Willie said, frowning. "I remember that woman. She used to sing in the church choir, and she used to have nothin' but high praise for Jack Trent."

"Guess the best way to find out's to ride out and see Ellie," Travis advised. "You been there, Willie. Lead the way."

Willie nodded and did just that. It took but a minute or two. All along the way people peered suspiciously from windows or behind wagons. When the visitors halted at the Trent house, someone threw a rock.

"You got sickness, go elsewhere!" a woman warned. "That doc's good for nothin' but buryin' folks!"

A second rock unsettled the big gray, and Willie had to fight to control the animal. He rode around back, dismounted, and tied the horse to an idle wagon. Travis and Mike followed suit. Then the three of them stepped to the back door and knocked lightly.

The door cracked open, and a slender boy of ten peeped out. His fingers gripped a cocked Remington revolver, and Willie drew back.

"Strange way to greet an old friend, William Trent,"

74

Willie scolded. "Ain't gone and forgot Wil Fletcher already, have you?"

"No. That you?" the boy asked, studying Willie's face.

"How 'bout you let me uncock that pistol?" Travis asked. "I'm your Uncle Travis up from Texas, and this here's your cousin Mike."

"Here," William said, passing the pistol to Travis. "That really you, Wil?"

"Ain't no other fool'd make the claim," Willie said, wrapping an arm around the youngster. "What's become o' your folks?"

"Pa's in surgery," the ten-year-old explained. "They call me Billy now, you know. Mr. Wyler's boy Joe had a horse fall on him, and Pa's settin' the leg. The Wylers is new, elsewise they'd not likely brought Joe here."

"What's happened?" Travis asked.

"Cholera," Billy whispered nervously. The word chilled the hall and left the three newcomers stone-faced.

It wasn't until later, after Dr. Jackson Trent had returned young Joe Wyler to his family, that Willie learned the rest of the dark tale. But even before that he sensed tragedy in the pale faces and restrained welcome extended Travis and Mike. Even the children—Billy and his brothers Cobb and Ellis, their sister Anne—were sullen and shy.

"Last summer we had a bad drought," Ellen said as she set a teakettle on the stove. "There were a lot of cattle at the river, Texas herds bound for Dodge mostly, and they fouled the shallows. Jack pleaded with the folks to boil their water or dig wells, but nobody listened. The cholera came late in the fall."

"There's a limit to what anyone can do once cholera starts up," Trent added. "I read up on treatments, and we tried near everything. I even found some Cheyennes and paid them to build a sweat lodge. That's when the people lost confidence."

"Strangely enough, it helped," Ellen said, drawing little

Anne onto one knee and rocking the six-year-old. "Billy and Ellis were wracked with fever, and the steam helped purge their systems. There was a woman, Viola Pennypacker, who accused us of practicing witchcraft, of saving our own children while we let the others die."

"We urged others to try the sweat lodge," Trent said, rubbing his eyes. "Miz Pennypacker and a band of her friends came out and burned the lodge. They found one of the Cheyennes and hung him. Afterward they died in droves, and those who could manage left Edwards. Some hauled their houses and stores along with them. Others just left. Half the town was gone by December. Back in February a fool went out of his head and set fire to the hotel. Miz Pennypacker lost her three youngsters about then, and she had her husband tear down the church. Then she took the fever herself in April and died."

"Was a blessing," Ellen said, sighing. "She was stirring people up, suggesting they come down and burn us out."

"I wonder why you stayed," Willie said, reading the sadness in their faces. "No future here now, and too much hatred for you to feel safe."

"Actually, we plan to leave," Ellen explained.

"We're going to Texas," Billy said, rushing over to a small table and fetching a handbill. He handed it over to Willie, who read with alarm.

ATTENTION

Needed in the town of Esperanza, Texas
ONE MARSHAL
ONE PREACHER
ONE DOCTOR
ONE TEACHER
FARM FAMILIES EAGER TO ENJOY PROSPER-
ITY
Address inquiries to Prudence Gunnerson,
Esperanza, Texas.

Will assist qualified persons with expenses.
Marshal, doctor, and teacher will receive land
and a house free of charge.

"I wrote the woman in May," Ellen said, cheering. "Just heard back from her. I'm to be the teacher, and Jack will practice medicine. It's a small town near the Salt Fork of the Brazos. The Brazos, Trav. The Brazos, Willie! I'm going home to Texas."

"It's not far from our ranch," Mike observed. "I go up there sometimes with the Slocums. Nice enough place, but poor."

"Mrs. Gunnerson says they'll enjoy a boom of prosperity due to ownership of the western cattle trail crossing of the river," Ellen said. "They can charge the herds a toll for . . ."

"We know," Travis said. "We come up that way, remember?"

"Ellen, there are plenty of Texas towns in need of a doctor," Willie said, frowning. "Choose another. I've met folks from Esperanza, and though they don't talk of it much, they're scared. This trail toll won't set lightly with cattlemen, they've had trouble. You know that country. The land's no good for farmin'. Can't be anything but bloodshed come of this. Haven't you fought your war?"

"More than once," she said sadly. "But the name of the place, Willie. Esperanza. In Spanish, it means hope! It's what I want for the children."

"You won't find it on the Salt Fork," Willie warned, and Travis added, "Amen."

"I already told Mrs. Gunnerson we'd come," Ellen told them. "And we will."

"It's a long, hard ride south to the Brazos," Travis said.

"I know," Ellen admitted. "I was counting on going back with you. You're a few days earlier than your letter suggested, and it will take us a day or so to pack our belongings. Then we'll leave, if that's all right?"

"Be good to have you back home," Travis said, walking over and embracing his sister.

"Be good to be home," Ellen countered. "I'm hungry for Texas."

"It's a rough trail to take with little ones," Willie cautioned as he gazed into the eager eyes of the children.

"Leastwise there won't be a pack of old crones tossing rocks at us," Billy mumbled. "Figure I can ride your horse, Wil?"

"No, I'd judge you to need a horse of your own," Willie answered. "You'll soon be a Texan, and Texans ride."

"We've got supply wagons at Dodge City and plenty of horses," Travis explained. "Tomorrow we'll bring them over."

"They'd be welcome," Trent said, lifting his chin. "I'll be glad to leave Edwards behind us."

"Have you sold the house?" Willie asked.

"No, and I won't," the doctor announced. "There's been too much sadness here. Better it's burned."

"Could fetch a decent price," Travis argued.

"From whom?" Trent asked. "This town's dead. Nobody pays money for the bones of a corpse."

"They'd burn it anyway after we left," Ellen declared. "We talked it over, and I won't have strangers picking at the things I have to leave. Cradles and beds, the children's names carved in the back door."

"Sometimes the past is best burned," Trent said, gazing intently at Willie. "Makes starting fresh all the easier."

"Maybe," Willie said, nodding sadly. But he knew coal oil and a torch wouldn't erase everything.

They were two days packing a lifetime's possessions into the two TS supply wagons Ted Slocum had generously turned over to Travis. A third day was spent converting the Trent's open bed wagon into a sort of caravan for the family. Plank beds were installed for Ellen, the doctor, and six-year-old Anne. The boys insisted on spreading blanket rolls cowboy-style with their cousin Mike.

"Got to get used to being Texans," Billy declared, and his brothers Cobb and Ellis readily agreed.

Once they set off southward, Willie tried to keep busy scouting the trail ahead or hunting game for the supper table. He didn't trust himself too long in Ellen's company. She stirred up too many memories. When she gripped his hand or smiled in his direction, the old fire burned within him, and he longed for something more.

"Sometimes I find myself wishin' Jack Trent wasn't such a good man," Willie confided to Travis. "Or that those angry Kansans had done somethin' more than toss stones."

"Yeah, I see the hurt," Travis said, nodding. "So does Ellie. She blames herself, you know."

"Was my doin', and I've told her as much."

"Well, she doesn't entirely believe that. It's hard for the both of us to see you so lost."

"I know where I am," Willie objected.

"And where you're goin'? No, Willie, you just stumble around like a stray pup, lookin' for somethin' you won't likely find."

"And what's that?"

"Belongin'."

The days spent camped along swollen rivers, watching the boys splash around in the shallows with their father, were a second trial.

"Hurts, doesn't it?" Ellen asked when she caught him gazing at the youngsters down on the North Canadian. "Could've been you."

"Should've been," he muttered. "If things had turned out different."

"You ought to find a good woman and settle down like Trav," she advised. "It's not too late for you to have a house full of kids."

"I came close a time or two," he confessed. "Each time a storm blew in and wrecked things. Was a little gal on the Sweetwater reminded me so much of you, and she didn't see the dark in my eyes."

"What happened to her?"

"Man come through and kilt her. Man I should've shot when I had the chance. Nowadays all I know's horses and blood. I put together a fair string each spring, you know. I half believe if I was left alone I could find peace raisin' those ponies. But sooner or later somebody'd come along and stir up trouble."

"Your brother Sam?"

"Oh, he thinks me dead and buried up in Colorado," Willie explained. "Maybe Willie Delamer *is* up there restin' under a stone marker."

"No, I knew him too well to believe that. When I look at you, I see the same boy I used to race across the river."

"No, I'm somebody different," he argued. "Killed too many men. Know what ole Yellow Shirt used to call me? Bright Star. Well, the brightness's all gone now, buried at Petersburg and Five Forks and a hundred places besides."

"Lots of men went to war, Willie. They've made their peace and built a new life."

"I never found any peace, though," he told her. "And none's come along."

After that talk, Willie noticed one or another of the Trent youngsters camping beside him each night.

"Mind if we call you Uncle Wil, like Mike does?" nine-year-old Cobb asked. "Ma said it was all right."

"Sure," Willie said, giving the child a hand with his blankets.

"Papa says maybe you'd take us hunting for rabbits tomorrow. Billy and me anyway."

"Could be," Willie said, staring at the boy's glistening blue eyes, at the long strands of flaxen hair that fell across his forehead. There was so much of Ellen in his face!

80

"You know, Ellis has a birthday coming along next week," Cobb added. "Billy was saying maybe you could help us make him a skin hat. I saw a coon prowling around last night."

"Could be. We'll see about it tomorrow."

"Coonskin cap'd be better than one made of rabbit fur. Rabbit's fine for a girl, but a boy ought to wear the hide of a coon, or maybe a wolf even."

"Not many wolves left, what with cowboys shootin' 'em up and down this trail. Scarcer'n buffalo in some parts."

"Coon'd do. Lots of them, don't you think?"

"We'll see," Willie promised.

So they set off next morning, Willie, Mike and the two older Trent boys. Mike shot a pair of rabbits and that night dropped a prowling racoon. Never mind who pulled the trigger. The Trent boys claimed the credit, and they did skin the rabbits and work the coonskin into a cap for their younger brother.

"It does my heart good to see you and the boys getting acquainted," Ellen told him when he set the rabbits on a spit.

"Tears at me, seein' so much of you in them."

"Too much might have been? Strange that you should see me in their faces. I always see you."

"Ellie, don't you see Jack?" he asked nervously.

"I see him in Anne. She's the image of her father, what with the dark hair and serious eyes. The boys, though, they've too much bull nettle and prickly pear to them."

He touched her shoulder, then stepped back.

"Better, I was a thousand miles away," he said, trembling.

"No, if what Trav says about Esperanza's true, we may have need of you."

"Sure, I'm handy when trouble's around."

"And welcome when it's not," she said, gently running her fingers along the side of his whiskered face.

"Ellie, you got a husband and little ones hereabouts," he said, retreating.

"I never forget that, Willie," she told him. "But I also remember the best friend I've ever known."

"And Jack?"

"He knows, Willie. Back in Edwards, when things were at their worst, he once told me it was a comfort to him, knowing that there was another man who loved me as much as he did, one who would do for me and the little ones."

"He's a good man, Ellie. Better'n me by half. Wish he wasn't sometimes, but there it is. Now I'd best get off and help those boys with Ellis's cap."

She reached out her hand, but he evaded it. He feared he would never be able to step away from her touch another time.

CHAPTER 10

The long trek south to Esperanza passed uneventfully. There was a brief visit with Lame Crow's Kiowas, and several encounters with South Texas herds headed to Kansas. Once, too, a band of riders trailed the wagons for an hour or so, but Willie dispatched them with a warning shot from his Winchester. There were better pickings elsewhere, after all.

Willie led the way into the growing string of buildings that Esperanza had become the final week of July. It was Sunday, and almost every family for fifteen miles had gathered at the new church the farmers had built across from Rupert Hamer's store.

"There are quite a lot of people here, aren't there?" Ellen observed.

"Lot of women and old people," Jack Trent added. "Plenty of youngsters. Not many men."

"War thinned 'em out," Willie explained. "Mostly Iowans. Young marrieds, old people, nigh-grown boys and girls."

Trent halted the lead wagon and fixed the brake. Travis stopped the second, and young Mike likewise arrested the third. A tall woman of generous proportions and commanding presence marched over, waving a quartet of teenage boys along.

"You folks look like you've come to stay," she observed.

"We have," Trent answered. "I'm Jackson Trent, physician by trade. Beside me here's my wife, Ellen, and my daughter Anne. Stuffed in that back supply wagon are our three boys."

"It's Dr. Trent and the teacher," the woman announced. "Saints be praised. None too soon so far's Agnes Fairchild's concerned, either."

A small woman heavy with child blushed, and the crowd laughed.

"I'm Prudence Gunnerson," the woman said, extending a large hand toward Dr. Trent. "We're pleased you've come. Matter of fact, we finished your house day before yesterday, and the barn's to go up Saturday next."

"Then we have a house to go to?" Ellen asked.

"Three miles north, near the river crossin'," Mrs. Gunnerson explained. "Best water for fifty miles. Started the well with my own hands. We figured it best the doc be close to the road, and it's handy to the schoolhouse, too."

"I think I'd like to go there directly, Jack," Ellen told her husband. "You might pick up some supplies here and join us."

"Store's not apt to be open Sunday," Trent pointed out.

"Dewey, you take these folks out to their house," a balding man suggested from the porch of the store. "Doc, that's my nephew Dewey there with the yellow hair, freckles, and ill-fittin' pants. Give him your list, and I'll see what you need's sent out directly. Name's Rupert Hamer, storekeeper. You can settle accounts when you have a mind."

"Dewey does know the way," Mrs. Gunnerson agreed. "Get to know that one. He's certain to be one of your challenges, Mrs. Trent. Gettin' him to sit still ten minutes for lessons is a test for Job's patience. He does know the country, though."

"Be happy to show you folks the house," Dewey said, loosening his string tie and scrambling out of a confining coat. "How you doin', Mr. Fletcher? That you, Mike? You got some color goin' to Kansas."

"You got some yourself," Mike responded. It was hard to tell which of the two had the whitest hair or the reddest nose. But it was Dewey's voice did the most croaking and cracking. That was no contest at all.

"Ready to head out, folks?" Dewey called as he mounted his beloved buckskin.

"We might at least meet some of our neighbors," Ellen pleaded.

"You will, too," Mrs. Gunnerson insisted. "We'll all of us come out and bring you some supper and a proper Esperanza welcome. Be food enough for an army and more chatter'n you've heard from all those menfolk in a month of Sundays!"

Willie watched the wagons make their slow turn back to the north and waved a brief farewell.

"You best come with us, Uncle Wil!" Mike called. "Lot o' work unpackin' these wagons."

"No, I think I'll check on my horses," Willie explained. "Be along in a day or two to see you've gotten settled."

"Willie?" Ellen called.

"Week at the most," he told her. "I'll tell Irene you and Mike are back," he added, nodding to Travis.

"Wouldn't want to miss out on the feed, Major," Dewey called, adopting the title in place of Willie's name. "Ma's sure to bake a peach pie."

"It's a temptation," Willie admitted, "but I've got horses to look to. Maybe another time."

He then turned the big gray south and galloped away. He heard Billy and Mike call his name, but he left their words to drift on the wind. Esperanza was Jack Trent's chance for a fresh start . . . and Ellen's. They didn't need him around to remind them of the past.

*   *   *

85

Willie was four days in the wilds beyond the Clear Fork of the Brazos when Travis and Jack Trent visited his camp.

"If you'd come a bit earlier, I would've had some coffee to offer you," Willie told them. "As it, I don't even have a cold biscuit for you to chew."

"Unless your cookin's gotten a lot better, we'd be safer chewin' mesquite thorns," Travis joked. "Didn't come to eat. Jack's got somethin' on his mind."

"Oh?" Willie asked.

"We're having a barn raising Saturday," the doctor explained. "Afterward there'll be a sort of celebration. Dancing and the like. Thought you might could do with a bit of cheering up."

"No, I feel just fine," Willie responded. "Got my horses, you know."

"The boys've missed you," Trent added. "Ellen, too."

"Look, Jack, I appreciate what you're sayin'. I know you and Ellie figure to owe me somethin' from the time I helped you out in Edwards. But bein' around her's, well, hard. Too many memories. Regrets."

"I know all about regrets," Trent said, dismounting. "And memories. I've got three dozen children dead in Edwards to haunt me the rest of my days. I hear the taunts of the townspeople, the screams of my own boys the night people came to my house and smashed all the windows. I put them through that!"

"Wasn't your doin'," Willie argued. "No, you can't blame yourself for people's fool ways."

"You would have strapped on a pistol and run them home."

"Or maybe shot three or four of 'em," Willie added. "Sure, that's a fine way. Killin' ain't a hard thing to do, you know. Body's just a bit of bone with some skin to cover the soft spots. It bleeds easy. A man can carve the life out of it without half tryin'. You, Jack, you got the gift to bring children into the world. To mend the tears men put in each

86

other or cure a fever. To my way of accountin', you stand well ahead of any tally I got in my favor."

"Willie, there's been some trouble in Esperanza," Travis said, sighing. "Somebody's run cows through some o' the fields, and the farmers're all up in arms."

"Well, they can't think it's you," Willie replied. "Or Ted."

"I don't suppose there's much thinking going on at all," Trent broke in. "Anyway, we got to talking it out, and I guess Ellen and I'd feel better if somebody was a little closer. It's a day's ride down here, you know."

"They've got a county sheriff in Throckmorton and a marshal in Esperanza," Willie pointed out.

"If trouble came, they'd be too far and too late," Travis muttered.

"I was just thinking how we have a corral you could use to work your horses and plenty of acres to roam if you tire of a roof over your head. But you'd be close."

"It's a lot to ask," Willie said, staring hard at the doctor. "More'n you can ever know."

"You're wrong, Wil. I'm the one man in this world who does know. I love Ellen, too."

"I'll think it over," Willie promised.

"We need you," Trent said as he stepped to his horse and climbed atop the saddle. "Ellen said to tell you that."

Willie paled. And as they rode away, he kicked a rock toward the river and uttered a curse. She knew he would come. He always would, too, if she asked. Even though it would hurt past reckoning.

As it turned out, Willie left most of the horses to graze beside the river. Lewis and Lamar were home from Kansas, and they would keep an eye on the animals. Willie headed north atop the gray, leading three ponies along behind him. They were nearly ready for saddles, and he'd work them at Jack Trent's corral.

He rode in on Saturday, so there was no trouble locating the place. Most of Throckmorton County was busy hammering pine planks into a barn, and Willie simply followed the noise. He drove the pintos into the corral, tied off the gray, and accepted a dipper of cool well water offered by Cobb Trent.

"Glad you came, Uncle Wil," the boy said. "Mama said you would. We're hungry for stories, you know."

"Figured after a week on the Salt Fork you'd have a few of your own," Willie said, grinning at the youngster.

"Well, Billy and I did spy the Kinsey sisters swimming in the river. Buff naked," he added with a red face.

"I expect your mama'll be hearin' about that," Willie said as he returned the dipper.

"Oh, nobody saw us," Cobb was quick to add. "Not this time anyway."

Cobb scrambled off to join a tangle of other boys, and Willie started toward the rising framework that was to become a barn. He got only halfway when Dewey Hamer galloped up, lathered and frantic.

"Lord, boy, what's got you riled?" his Uncle Rupert called.

"Uncle Rupe, you seen Ernst or Wolf?" Dewey cried.

"No, they were comin' with you, I thought," the storekeeper answered.

"They're gone! Dewey exclaimed. "Taken off."

"What?" the people cried. "Taken where?"

"Calm yourself, Dewey," Mrs. Gunnerson commanded. "Tell us what's happened."

"I was supposed to go by Uncle Sime's farm and fetch my cousins," Dewey explained as he fought to catch his breath. "They weren't there. Oh, the tools were in the field, all right, and one of Wolf's shoes, too. Horse tracks and trampled corn plants."

"I saw a couple of riders," Jacob Taylor declared. "They looked to be carrying something across their saddles. I didn't think much about it, but it could have been those boys."

"What riders?" Mrs. Gunnerson demanded. "Where?"

"Men dressed like cowboys," Taylor explained. "One ridin' a big brown horse and the other a spotted sort."

"Webb Scarlet rides a brown horse," Rupert Hamer pointed out. "I'll bet that's who's done it."

"But why?" Taylor asked.

"I know," Dewey said, his face turning pale. "Were some cows in the fields this week, and we chased 'em to the river. One of 'em got itself trapped in a bog and broke a leg. Later on that Webb Scarlet and one of his brothers came and got it out. They had to shoot it in the end. Uncle Sime got into some serious yellin' with 'em."

"And just where is Simon now?" Mrs. Gunnerson asked.

"Gone to Albany for plow blades," Rupert Hamer answered. "So it was just the boys home."

"What'll they do to 'em?" Dewey asked. "Ern's just thirteen, and Wolf's but eleven."

"Best we notify the marshal," Taylor declared. "I'll ride to town and tell him."

"What will we do if we find them, Dewey?" his Uncle Rupert asked. "Have a gun battle with those cowboys? You can maybe challenge Webb Scarlet? He's killed men."

"Your uncle's right," Willie said, stepping over beside Dewey. "You folks go ahead and tell the marshal. Meanwhile, maybe Dewey and I'll have a look."

"That's for me to do," Dewey argued. "But I guess it wouldn't hurt if you rode along. I don't mind company."

"Sure," Willie said, grinning. "After all, those cousins of yours might've wandered down the river a way, maybe took a swim."

"They didn't," Dewey argued.

"And if you track them to the Scarlets?" Mrs. Gunnerson asked. "You're not the sheriff or even a town marshal."

"No, but I've got a knack for convincin' fellows to do what's right," Willie told her. "Could be them Scarlets might not be so unreasonable as you might think. To their thinkin', they've been wronged. Trick's findin' a way to right that wrong and get those boys back."

"You ought to have company," Trent suggested. "Three would stand a better chance."

"Or seven," Mrs. Gunnerson added.

"No, just Dewey and me," Willie said. "I'd go alone except I wouldn't know those cousins from a pair of wild pigs. And anyway, Dewey wouldn't let me. Come on, son. Let's saddle a couple of fresh horses and have ourselves a ride."

Jack Trent furnished a pair of roan mares, and it took only a few minutes for Willie to slide his saddle off the gray and onto one of the mares. Dewey was even faster, and the two of them set off down the river immediately thereafter. They passed the Kinsey place and found Simon Hamer's farm just beyond it. The scene was much as Dewey had described it, and there was a clear trail left by two heavily burdened horses through the river bottom and past Jacob Taylor's farm.

"You think this is the right trail?" Dewey asked when they passed several other sets of tracks heading north and south.

"I judge those to be riders, true enough, but the ones we're followin' have to be carryin' extra loads. See how deep the hoofprints are? We're on the right trail, sure enough."

"We're headin' right for the Scarlet house," Dewey said, trembling. "Be there in two, three miles. What do we do when we get there?"

"Talk," Willie explained. "Thing is, by their reckonin', they got a grievance. Your cousins ran their beeves and as good as killed one of 'em. They may want to be paid for it. Could be they'll ask money for your cousins."

"I never heard o' Bob Scarlet askin' for money," Dewey mumbled. "But I seen plenty o' men beat and one shot even for causin' him trouble."

"If he'd wanted to shoot those boys, he'd've done it at the river, so you'd take it for a warnin'. No, he's got somethin' else in mind."

Knowing that didn't make the job ahead any easier though. Dewey led the way toward a long plank house nestled in a rocky notch in the hillside, and Willie edged his right hand a hair closer to the Colt resting on his right hip.

"Hold up there!" a voice called, and Dewey halted his horse. Willie rode a bit farther, then turned toward a clump of junipers.

"That you, Randy?" Willie asked. "Ain't you eager to greet an old friend."

"No, he ain't," Webb Scarlet answered, emerging from the trees at Randy's side. A Sharps carbine rested in Webb's hands, and a grim smile appeared on his lips.

"What business you got here, Fletcher?" Bob demanded as he stepped out of the house. Two small children huddled beside a woman in the doorway.

"Haven't met your little ones, Bob," Willie said, softening a hair. "Might be you'll understand how a body can get worried when a boy or two wanders off. Dewey here's missin' a couple o' cousins. They seem to've jumped atop some horses and ridden out here. I thought you might help me find 'em."

"What would these boys be to you?" Bob asked.

"Just boys," Willie answered. "I'd have a look after your little ones if they strayed. Call it a soft heart I got. Anyway, I'd be obliged if you could turn 'em over."

"Ain't got 'em," Webb barked. "Now get off our land."

"Got title to this place, do you?" Willie asked. "Well, that'd be a matter for the law. Me, I just come to take those boys home."

"And I said . . ."

"No, you must've been mistaken," Willie interrupted as he gazed toward a small shed. A pair of overalls was draped over a bench there, and beside them rested a straw hat.

"That's Ern's hat," Dewey whispered.

"You wouldn't be callin' me a liar, would you?" Webb asked as he stepped closer to the shed. Willie slid off his horse and stepped sideways to the shed's door. Keeping watch on Webb's carbine all the while, Willie kicked open the shed. A pair of yellow-haired boys stumbled out. Their hands were bound, and their mouths were gagged. They'd been stripped to their drawers, and the sharp red stripes left by a lash painted their bare backs.

"Like I said, you made a mistake," Willie fumed as he drew out a knife and cut the boys loose. "Care to explain yourself?"

"I never explained anything in my whole life!" Bob shouted.

"Try, why don't you," Willie said, glaring at the Scarlets while Dewey climbed down to help his cousins collect their clothes and recover their wits.

"They rode down on us in our fields, mister!" little Wolf cried. "Dragged us here and whipped us bad. We told 'em we didn't mean their cow should break a leg, said we'd pay for it even, but they just went on whippin' us."

"Trust it was a lesson well learned," Bob growled.

"Lesson?" Willie asked, staring at the cowering youngsters. "I seen marks like that before, Bob Scarlet. What you do to your brothers is one thing, but you've no right to hurt these kids. I expect the law'll want to talk to you about it."

"All kinds o' laws, Fletcher," Webb said, cocking his rifle. "Like trespassin'."

Willie whipped out his pistol and fired a shot past Webb's ear. The rifle discharged harmlessly, and Webb dropped it as he staggered back, shaken.

"You point a gun at me again, I'll kill you," Willie warned. "Would have this time only I got acquainted with your brothers on the trail, and I bear you no general grudge. Now, Bob, you figure to still have an account to settle here? Or is beatin' small boys all the satisfaction you need?"

"They kilt my cow!" Bob shouted. "Fool farmers'll ruin the country. They got no business here!"

"They own the land," Willie argued. "If you'd talked to 'em, they might've made good your loss. You keep this up, you'll be at war."

"I am at war!" Bob yelled. "Have been since Fort Sumter. Been pushed west till I lost all patience for laws or people, either one. This is my land now, not because it says so in any book, but because I plan to hold it. You settin' yourself up opposite me, Fletcher? You got that big a wish to die?"

"Do you?" Willie asked. "Because you haven't imagined the sort of nightmare crossin' my path would bring you. Try it and find out!"

"Fletcher!" Bob shouted as Willie helped each of the Hamer boys in turn up onto a roan mare.

"Tell brother Jim to use that rifle or rest it easy," Willie called as he mounted up. "I see him in the rocks yonder, and I'll kill him if he wants."

"Jim, put the gun away," Bob ordered. "We'll be meetin' again, Fletcher."

"Sure we will," Willie said, nodding to Randy as he backed his horse from the Scarlet ranch.

Willie and Dewey rode to Esperanza and left the cousins to relate their tale to Wade Maddock, who had taken on the job of town marshal. The marshal was still settling into his office at the new jail.

"Come the trial, I'll want your testimony, too," the marshal told Willie. "To findin' 'em in the shed and all."

"Dewey was there," Willie grumbled. "He can tell it plain enough."

"I'll have an easier time gettin' warrants from a judge with your statement. Write it out, won't you?"

"You figure to arrest 'em?" Willie asked. "By yourself, I expect. You really want a war?"

"If it comes to that, I'm prepared to fight," Maddock said. "These Scarlets have been all over. They drift in, stir up a fuss, and move on when the law sets itself on their

93

trail. Once they see I mean business, they'll settle down. Or head elsewhere.''

"I don't seem 'em doin' either," Willie argued. "You didn't see the eyes o' the young ones. Bob's woman. Here's folks that've been pushed a ways—hard. Might could be nasty mad already. Push 'em, and they'd be downright dangerous.''

"They didn't shoot you."

"I fished Thad and Randy from Pease River. Might be they consider I've had that debt paid now, though. I plan to be careful. You do the same."

"I'll note the warnin', Fletcher," the marshal answered. "And the statement?"

"You still need it, I'll scribble somethin' down next time I come to town."

But as it happened, there was no need.

"Ern and Wolf changed their stories," Dewey explained the next week when Willie came across the boy down at the river.

"Oh?" Willie asked.

"Was a fire in Uncle Sime's toolshed. In the ashes was a board branded SCAR. Ain't hard to figure it would've been the barn next and afterward the house. Marshal Maddock was talkin' jail time, and Bob Scarlet passed word around he wouldn't stand for such. He's got folks mighty scared, you know. Even old soldiers like Uncle Sime. I never figured him one to run from a fight."

"Soldiers know what a war's like," Willie countered. "Not much glory to it. Just blood and death. It's a thing a man should turn from."

"You didn't."

"Well, I done few smart things in my life, Dewey. And rilin' Bob Scarlet wasn't one of 'em."

CHAPTER 11

Willie settled in at the Trent place and tried to ignore the growing enmity between farmers and cattlemen. That wasn't easy. When neighbors dropped by to gaze at the new barn or to visit with Ellen and Jack, he felt hostile eyes fall upon his rough leather boots and his buckskin trousers. There was the hard, windblown life etched in Willie's features. After all, he was most days working his range ponies or off hunting down game for the supper table.

"Got to do something to earn my keep," he remarked.

"You earn it," Jack assured him.

Willie supposed it was true. Each night before falling between his blankets atop the narrow slat bed he'd installed in the barn, Willie walked the river, searching the dusty road for fresh tracks. Often he arose from a light sleep to investigate a horse's shudder or a squawking goose. Mostly it proved to be a prowling bobcat or a skunk sniffing around the woodpile. Once a shadowy horseman did splash across the river and disappear.

"Uncle Wil could sure sleep better if we got ourselves a dog," Billy said when Willie contented himself the intruder had left for good.

"Oh, I expect he'd have himself a look anyway," Trent

said, nodding to Willie from the porch. "He's that way, you know."

"Sure, but a dog'd be handy just the same," the boy argued.

So Willie talked Ted Slocum out of a floppy-eared hound, and the Trent youngsters had their dog.

"You haven't noticed any cattle on those farms up in Esperanza, have you?" Ted asked when Willie visited the ranch to pick up the animal.

"Some," Willie noted. "A few of those folks drove in longhorn cows a year or so back, and they've bred a few animals. Most everybody has dairy cows."

"None with a TS brand, though."

"Can't say I've been close enough to see, Ted. Missin' some beeves?"

"Yes, and we're not the only ones. Most every outfit's spied riders. At first they were just renegade hiders up from Fort Griffin or down from the Nations."

"But you've changed your mind?" Willie asked.

"Hiders come in and hit fast. Then they're gone. Whoever's responsible for the missin' stock's takin' twenty, thirty head every week or so but rarely any more. Be easy to hide a few dozen animals with a small herd of legal ones."

"You're talking about rustlers."

"I am. Twenty head mount up after a time, too. Oh, it's not killin' me or Trav, but people like Albert Henley are stirred up. He and Peters, some of the others, have formed an association of sorts."

"Thinkin' of hirin' a range detective?" Willie asked nervously.

"Talked on it some," Ted confessed. "Costs money, though, and they don't have the cash. Good help isn't cheap, you know."

"I know all too well."

"Major, blood's hot, and fevers are runnin' high for ridin' north and callin' some farmers to account. They've got that Bob Scarlet to stir them up."

"Plan on whippin' some more farm kids, does he?" Willie asked angrily.

"Could be farmers behind this. If it is, I don't suppose they'll be stoppin' with a bullwhip."

"No, not if Scarlet's takin' a hand."

"Major, you're up there in the middle o' those folks. If you had a good look, spoke to farmers maybe . . ."

"And told them you suspect they're stealing?" Willie cried. "That would make me popular. Have you spoken to Wade Maddock?"

"Scarlet says he's the farmers' paid badge, and there's some truth to that, too. Won't Henley or Peters trust him to deal with this."

"I'll have a look, Ted. And I'll pass on what you've told me to Jack Trent. He's been through a fight and knows how to talk to folks. They'd listen to a doctor, too. These folks respect education."

"And if things don't get better, you keep your head down. Trouble's on the wind."

"Yes, I smell it," Willie admitted. "There's bad blood up north, too. You should see the looks I get sometimes."

"Don't get caught on the wrong side of the lines, Major."

"And you help me see it doesn't come to any lines, Ted. We've had enough war for three lifetimes."

"Suppose we have at that."

True to his word, Willie did speak with Jack Trent. The doctor listened attentively before frowning his reply.

"I'll talk to Mrs. Gunnerson, Wil, but the truth is that most of these people are too busy getting ready for harvest to be behind the kind of trouble you're talking about. For one thing, where would they get the horses? You don't suppose these rustlers are stealing stock on foot, do you?

"There's a bigger problem, though. Cattle wander this country at will, trampling crops, grazing on cornstalks, and driving good people to extraordinary lengths to protect their property and children. It would be rubbing an open sore to confront these very people with such an accusation as the one you've brought me."

"Don't present it as a charge," Willie advised. "Just tell 'em of the problem. Shoot, rustlers'll steal their stock, too. The real danger's that the clearheaded folk might follow Bob Scarlet on some sort of revenge raid. Be people die if it comes to that."

"That's true," Trent said, sighing. "And I know what's in your heart. Still . . ."

"Just talk to 'em, Jack. Tell 'em to keep their eyes open and to be careful for a time. I can't forget Dewey's little cousins, and they shouldn't, either. A man who'd whip little boys is sure to surprise you some more."

Willie, meanwhile, had a look around Esperanza for the missing cattle. Ellen made two trips into town to insure the schoolhouse was ready for classes to begin after harvest. Willie rode along as a sort of escort for her and the little ones. While Billy, Cobb, and Ellis helped their mother nail shelves together and set up curtains on the windows—or tend little Anne—Willie galloped off across the country. On other occasions he would visit the Hamers or share some tale with a band of children taking a cooling break from the oppressive August heat down at the river.

"Ever notice anybody runnin' cattle around here?" Willie often asked. "From the south up through town maybe."

"Sometimes," Ernst Hamer said once. "Didn't recognize 'em, though. They were with one of those Scarlet brothers."

"Wasn't SCAR brands on the cows, though," Wolf pointed out.

"Was on the horses, though," Ern insisted. "That mean one, Webb, was along last time."

Willie digested the words slowly. He tried not to betray his anger. It would be like Bob Scarlet to steal his neighbors' stock, wouldn't it? He'd done so before. And to blame the farmers, well, that would serve even better.

When Willie told Ted Slocum, the rancher shook his head in dismay.

"Not sayin' it ain't so, Major, but I can't tell the others some farm boy's pointed the finger at Bob Scarlet. Especially not them two. Was Bob whipped 'em, and there's a fine grudge there. Besides, it was the Scarlets caught one batch red-handed."

"What?" Willie cried.

"Had fifteen beeves, mostly Diamond H brand, headed for Throckmorton."

"And the rustlers?"

"Three out-of-work cowboys off a South Texas trail herd, a Fort Griffin renegade named Polk Lawrence, and a young fellow name of Dowe."

"I've heard of Lawrence," Willie muttered. "Old buff hunter. He's near sixty, I'd guess, and lame to boot."

"Was smart enough to steal cattle most of the summer," Ted pointed out. "The others are younger."

"How much younger?"

"That Dowe boy's not as old as Lewis, and a hair shy of bein' as tall. Major, his pa's got a farm on Salt Fork."

"That'll go hard," Willie said, nervously shifting his feet.

"They've got the five of 'em locked up in the storeroom of Walin's store. Trial's supposed to be next week sometime, but it's no use. They had the cattle and runnin' irons, too. Be hangin' come of it."

"You think there'll even be a trial?" Willie asked, nodding toward the corral where Webb Scarlet sat watching Walin's back door. "Henley's a hothead by nature, and there are others quick to rile."

"With reason, I'd say," Ted argued. "Trial or no trial, Bob Scarlet'll be for settlin' accounts with Dowe's pa. Bob's got a talent for burnin' down things, as I hear it."

"Seems to favor fire."

"Maybe I ought to send a couple of men up to help you tend your horses."

"They wouldn't be made to feel welcome," Willie replied. "Some of these farmers might take it as a threat and go off half-cocked."

"You could be right. Anyhow, you sleep light and take care. I got downright used to havin' you around. As for Lamar and Lewis, well, they figure you're family."

"Wouldn't care to see my hide peppered with lead, eh? Well, I wouldn't, either."

Willie had a terrible sense of foreboding as he rode homeward. He might have kept his thoughts to himself had not Dewey Hamer chosen that day to visit his uncle in Esperanza. As Willie passed Rupe Hamer's little store, Dewey called out.

"Howdy, Major!" Dewey said as he trotted alongside Willie's horse. "Been down to the Salt Fork lately? I thought to have a swim later on."

"Not today," Willie muttered. The glow melted from Dewey's face, and the fifteen-year-old grew solemn.

"Trouble?" he asked.

"Might be," Willie confessed. "Ever hear of a boy named Dowe, Dewey?"

"Couple of 'em," Dewey said, growing worried.

"Be about your age."

"It's Cory then," Dewey concluded. "Ain't see him much this summer. Strange, considerin' his pa's got a big place and just Cory and Cully to help. Cully's only twelve, too, no bigger'n Wolf."

"Cory's got himself jailed in Throckmorton," Willie explained. "Charged with stealin' cattle."

"Then he's a dead man," Rupert Hamer declared as he walked over. "They'll wait for the circuit judge, and cattle money pays his bills. Can't be Cory's back of this, Mr. Fletcher. Boy's simple."

"He's got company," Willie announced. "Three cowboys and an old man who used to hunt buffalo."

"Will they let Cory off, him bein' young and all?" Dewey asked.

"Not likely," Willie answered. "Way folks figure things, if a fellow's old enough to steal, he's old enough to hang."

"Might give him a jail sentence though," Rupert added.

"Know any jails hereabouts?" Willie asked. "They send him south, he wouldn't live long anyhow. Boy that age in Huntsville? No, hangin's quick at least."

"He's my friend," Dewey whispered. "When we first come here, wasn't many boys. Major, he's not smart the way some people hold proper, but he's not stupid either. He wouldn't steal cows without somebody puttin' him up to it. Or forcin' him."

"How long's it been since you two skipped rocks in the river, Dewey?" Rupert asked.

"A while," the boy admitted.

"People change, nephew. I heard about some boys bein' caught, and it's said they had the stock and branding irons besides. They haven't even claimed innocence, as I hear it. Best you save your sympathy for the rest of us. There are those who figure if Cory's involved, the whole of Esperanza's practiced thievery as well."

"He's right," Dewey declared. "Guess I best ride up and holler at Miz Gunnerson. And tell Mr. Dowe. I expect he doesn't know himself. Cory can't write, you see."

"Trial's set for Wednesday next," Rupert announced. "Heard Marshal Maddock say that."

"I'll pass it on to Mr. Dowe. Major, you think maybe you could ride into Throckmorton with us Wednesday? If I can get leave from my chores, I'd want to be at the trial. Maybe Cory's gone and changed, but you ought to stand by your friends when they're up against hard times, don't you think?"

"Better not to borrow trouble, Dewey," his uncle warned.

"I'll ride along," Willie agreed. "But don't go suggestin' to Farmer Dowe he ought to come. Feelings'll be runnin' high, and he could come to regret that trip. Better go in to see his boy earlier and by night. Marshal might take him."

"Suggest it," Rupert agreed. "Safer all around. No need for Charlie Dowe to bring an army of cowboys riding down on us like Comanches on the warpath."

Dewey nodded his agreement, then hurried over to fetch his pinto. Willie accompanied the young man as far as the river.

"Don't much envy you your job," Willie confessed as Dewey turned toward the Dowe farm.

"No, sir, but it'd come better from me than strangers. And better 'fore they go and hang Cory."

Willie nodded, then left Dewey to his task. He rode on to the Trent place and shared the news with Ellen and Jack.

"Wednesday's the trial?" Trent asked. "You don't think the stockmen would do anything stupid before then, would you?"

"If those Scarlets are involved, I'm surprised they haven't lynched the Dowe boy and those cowboys already!" Ellen cried. "Jack, you should call the people together."

"Why him?" Willie asked.

"That's your doing," the doctor explained. "When I started speaking to folks about those thefts and the trouble they could cause, everyone got together and voted me mayor. Mayor? What's Esperanza need with a mayor? Anyway, I was plenty content to let Grandma Gunnerson rule the roost."

"Others thought differently," Ellen added, resting her cheek against her husband's shoulder.

"I think they feel, being a doctor and married to the sister of a cattleman, I might be in less danger."

"That's not true," Willie pointed out. "No more here than it was in Edwards. It's a fool sticks his neck out, Jack."

"Hear that, Ellen?" Trent asked. "Is this the man who

rode into Edwards and risked his hide for our sake? And who's sleeping in our barn to keep watch over us by night?''

"It is sort of the pot calling the kettle black, Willie," she noted.

"Was a fire scorched the both of 'em," Willie pointed out. "And if the right words stir the right folks up, come Wednesday there could be enough fire hereabout to scorch half of Texas."

"Maybe we should make a show of force in Throckmorton," Ellen suggested. "Call out the Esperanza militia. It might encourage the judge to be more fair-minded."

"Militia?" Willie asked. "See any of them step forward when the Hamer boys vanished?"

"They disbanded when Maddock arrived," Trent explained.

"Somebody should go," Ellen argued.

"Sure, Ellie, hold Anne on your lap," Willie muttered in dismay. "It won't save that boy from a rope if they caught him with stolen beeves. And hangin' can fire a mob faster'n anything I know. Stay home and bolt your shutters."

"She's right, though," Trent added, "Somebody ought to go, just to see what happens and let us know."

"I'll be there," Willie told them. "Promised Dewey to ride with him. I'll do my best to talk that boy out of bein' such a fool, but if he goes, so will I."

"And if he doesn't?" Ellen asked.

"I'll get word to Ted and Trav. They'll have a man attend the trial, and we'll get the word from him."

"I can't help feeling like we're caught in the middle of this fight," Ellen said, sighing. "My whole family's on one side, but these people have been so kind. I want to see that little school filled with children, and I long to see this valley bloom with prosperity. The open range can be so bleak, after all."

"Sure," Willie agreed. "Bein' in the middle's no way to face a war, though, Ellie. It's a sure way to catch a bullet one way or the other."

CHAPTER 12

Willie did his best to dissuade Dewey Hamer from riding to Throckmorton for the trial, but the boy was mule stubborn and wouldn't change his mind.

"I just figure there ought to be somebody there who's not hungry to see a hangin'," Dewey declared. Willie had a hard time disputing it, even if he knew it was a fool's errand and dangerous to boot.

The trial itself lasted but an hour. Three witnesses testified to having seen the five accused driving stolen cattle, and there were the running irons for the jury to see. Not one of the twelve men hadn't run stock on the open range, and their eyes widened with anger when the state attorney showed how easy it was to change one brand to another with those irons.

As for the rustlers, only Polk Lawrence made much effort to defend himself.

"We was only hired to move the stock," the old buffalo hunter pleaded.

"By whom?" the lawyer asked.

"Don't know his real name. Called himself French George. I met him when I was huntin' buffs out of Fort Griffin. I hired on these youngsters for spare hands. Lord,

104

they didn't know we were runnin' stolen beeves, nor did I.''

"Guess you happened upon them runnin' irons by accident," Bob Scarlet called from the back of the room.

"I swear I never seen them before in my life!'' Lawrence claimed. "Must be that fellow stopped us had 'em.''

"I'm sure the cattlemen had reason to steal their own stock,'' Judge Hiram Kramer said, shaking his head. "Have you any witnesses, Mr. Lawrence? Did anyone know of this meeting in Fort Griffin?''

"Any that did won't talk,'' Lawrence admitted. "I guess if I was in your place, judge, I'd be for hangin'. Only five men's words they didn't steal, and it ain't much in a country famous for liars. I'd just strike this deal with you and the folks yonder,'' Lawrence added, turning to the jurors. "Me, I'm an old man who's earned hangin' a hundred times. But these others, and especially Cory there who doesn't hardly know what's happenin', maybe deserve a measure o' mercy. String me up to pay for the inconvenience I caused, but let them others slide by, won't you?''

There was a hint of sympathy in the eyes of Judge Kramer, and one of the jurors nodded. Scarlet saw and let fly a speech on the ruination of stockraisers. There was a loud murmur of agreement, and the softness left the faces of the jurors.

The deciding took but an instant, and all five were declared guilty. It was for the judge to decide sentence, and he ordered the whole batch hung next dawn.

"Well, everybody knew it,'' Bart Peters told Willie outside the courthouse. "Judge Kramer travels with the state attorney and a hangman. Likely they'll use them tall oaks back of Walin's store. Ain't another spot high enough to do the job and won't anybody pay for a gallows.''

"No, money's tight, I guess,'' Willie observed.

"Who's this fence rail you got with you here?'' Peters went on to ask. "Not Ellie's boy surely.''

"Dewey Hamer, meet Bart Peters,'' Willie said, nudging the boy forward. "He grew up with the Dowe boy and thought to offer what comfort a friendly face might provide.''

"Sure. I'd figure a rustler deserves a rope, but I'd not've argued much if they'd let that one go. He clear don't know cows from cannons, and he's not pocketed much cash from thievin'. If he wasn't farm-raised, likely Scarlet would have spoke for lettin' him go, but that bunch is lockjaw set against plow scratchers.''

Willie nodded and then tried to edge Dewey along to where their horses were tied. They got but a few feet when Webb Scarlet blocked the path.

"Now, there's another o' them farmers!'' Webb declared. "And that Fletcher fellow who sides with 'em. Maybe we ought to get some more rope for that hangman.''

"Figure it's a crime to be a farmer, do you?'' Willie asked. "Or do Scarlets just try to get a judge to do what they don't figure they can do themselves?''

"I'm ready here and now to settle accounts with you,'' Webb claimed, slapping the Colt resting on his hip and squaring off.

"Ain't the time, Webb,'' Bob barked. "Friends, you give me a listen. There may be some who figure me hardhearted to argue for hangin' them five, especially the boy, but you've all lost stock to thieves, and you know the loss hits deep and hard. Especially when you're gettin' started in a new country. Me and my brothers made many a fresh start. Had to. Our folks were kilt by Yankees! Pa durin' the war and Ma after. We had our land taken by taxin' carpetbaggers again and again. Chased us from one place to the other.

"Come to Throckmorton County only to find new hardships. We filed on land, built us a house, and then these farmers come along and claim title. People shoot our beeves or chase 'em into river bogs. Now this stealin'. Shoot, I fought Yanks and Indians and outlaws to hold my land and my stock. Got a little brother buried on the trail to Kansas and two more lyin' east, kilt by Comanche arrows. Ain't any softness left in me, not for farm boys turned thieves nor anybody else who'd steal what's mine.

"Now I ask you this. Most o' you folks's is no different from me. You ain't got thousands o' acres nor cows neither like TS Ranch or the Cobb outfit out on Clear Fork. Each cow counts. We leave these farmers to steal our property or crowd us out from water, and we'll all o' us go the way o' the buffalo. You eager for the day when your sons and daughters' skulls dot this range? Not me! Who's for ridin' to Esperanza and bein' done with these Yankee cow-killers?"

"Hold on now!" Willie shouted. "I know about that cow that got kilt, and it wasn't the boy's fault who chased it off his corn. A man tends his stock, and when it strays he ought to ride out and bring it home. He leaves it to wander forever, it's just good sense his neighbor's got to protect his fields. I've chased a steer or two out of a garden, and I'd wager the rest o' you have, too. As for ownin' the land up Esperanza way, as I hear it those farmers've been there ten years. When did you show up, Bob Scarlet?"

"You know I'm right!" Scarlet yelled. "Don't let this weak-stomached fool trick you with his words. That's one o' them farmers there with him!"

Willie started to voice a reply, but he swallowed the words instead. The eyes of the others turned hostile, and he felt their hot gaze on his brow.

"Get mounted and ride along home," Willie whispered to Dewey. "Best we get along."

"Yes, you best!" Webb Scarlet agreed.

"We got no grudge against you, Major," Bart Peters explained. "We all know where your heart is. But we got somethin' to tend to, and it's best you not find yourself in the way."

"And if I do?" Willie asked.

Webb tapped his pistol, and the others murmured their agreement.

"Be a sad day I have to shoot bullets into you boys,"

Willie said as he climbed atop his big gray. "You come north on business, make sure you've got warrants and laws in your favor. Especially if you ride along Salt Fork."

"Ain't he the one for tall words," Bob Scarlet declared.

"Ain't bad at backin' 'em," Peters noted. "You been to Kansas with him, Scarlet. I wouldn't want him on the other side."

"What other side?" Bob asked. "There's no sides here. Just us, our God-given rights, and a bunch of fool farmers who can either run back north or . . ."

Willie didn't hear the last part, for he was too busy kicking his horse into motion. He knew the sentiment well enough though. He and Dewey rode north at a gallop. They both felt the hot breath of trouble pursuing their every step.

Willie left Dewey in town and rode on to the Trent place. He half expected Bob Scarlet to come riding up, waving a torch and shouting curses that very day. As it happened, Scarlet and his cronies were too busy celebrating the verdict with whiskey and preparing for the hanging to bother anybody just then.

The day after Polk Lawrence, Cory Dowe, and the three cowboys were dispatched to their respective graves, Willie was down at the river with Ellen's boys. They'd gone to wash away the August weariness and snag a catfish or two for supper, and Willie was enjoying their antics.

"When're you coming in, Uncle Wil?" Billy called from time to time. The grin Billy flashed at his younger brothers warned of a plot, and Willie eased himself a step or two farther back from the river. Cobb sent a handful of water that way, and Ellis laughed.

"I'll race you to the hollow oak!" Cobb offered. "If you don't think you're too old."

"Old enough to drown a Brazos river rat like you," Willie answered.

He started to kick off his boots, then stopped. His ears

picked up the unmistakable noise of horses splashing through the shallows downstream, and he instantly motioned the boys to shore.

"Uncle Wil?" Billy cried.

"Back behind those trees there," Willie said, pointing to a stand of willows. "Hurry."

Billy led his brothers to shore. They grabbed their clothes and followed Willie's finger to cover. Willie meanwhile lifted a Winchester brought along for the purpose and prepared to confront the approaching riders.

There were three of them. One was a young Diamond H hand, Hank Sibley. One was a stranger. Their leader was Randolph Scarlet.

"Afternoon, Randy," Willie called. "What brings you out this way?"

"Lookin' for strays," the young man answered.

"Won't find any here," Willie answered. "Never knew a cow to wander through here."

"Not on its own anyhow," Randy observed. "Some have help, you know. There's all sorts of strays, too. Been farm boys to get lost and find their way onto our land. Me and the boys here try to set 'em straight."

"You go along with that, Hank?" Willie called.

"I do what Mr. Henley bids me," Hank replied. " 'Cept for usin' a lash. I ain't for that, no, sir, Major."

"I suppose you Scarlets got a special affection for rawhide whips, eh, Randy?" Willie asked.

"They do a fair job of teachin'," Randy answered.

"Good as Pease River?"

"No, nor a steer's horn neither. Ain't Thad or me forgot what you done there," Randy declared. "Might be better if you moved back south of the Clear Fork, though. Safer there."

"Never was partial to safe places," Willie said, frowning as the Trent boys eased their way closer to his side.

"Ain't altogether friendly holdin' that rifle on us," Hank noted.

"Just lookin' after my concerns," Willie told them.

"Well, Bob says we've got no quarrel with the doc as of yet," Randy said, waving his companions back down the river. "But it might be better if you didn't do any strayin' yourself, say down toward old man Dowe's place. We keep mighty watchful around there."

"I appreciate the warnin'."

"Like I say," Randy concluded, "I figure to owe you. But watch your back. Ain't everybody looks at it that way."

Willie nodded his understanding. As Randy Scarlet galloped off to join his companions, Willie relaxed his grip on the Winchester and turned to the boys.

"Billy, I guess that's all the swimmin' for today," Willie said, scowling. "Get along home now."

"You comin', Uncle Wil?" Cobb asked.

"In a bit," Willie answered. "Plan to watch the river awhile. You tell your mama we had company. Best she and your papa know."

"Yes, sir," Billy said, leading his brothers up the hill toward the house.

Willie sat beside the river nearly an hour. Until he saw the smoke. At first he sniffed out a hint of coal oil in the wind. Then he spied the black cloud curling skyward a mile or two downriver.

"You see it, too, eh?" Jack Trent called as he led his roan mare and Willie's gray toward the river. "I judge it's Grandma Gunnerson's farm. Or the Dowe place next over. Somebody's set the field afire."

"Or maybe the house," Willie said as he accepted his horse's reins and prepared to mount. "Might be better if you stayed. It could be Bob Scarlet's finally worked up the stockmen into a fever."

"If that was true, you'd hear them," Trent argued as he mounted his animal. "If Scarlet's paid a call, it's more likely somebody'll need me than they will you."

"Maybe so," Willie conceded. "Keep close and stay

back if I signal you. And if you know any prayers, say one for us all."

They splashed into the river then and galloped along toward the smoke. As they closed the distance, Willie saw Trent had been right. Grandma Gunnerson's northeast acreage was ablaze. A small army of farmers was fighting the fire with wet blankets and shovels, driving the flames toward the river and cutting it off from the adjacent fields.

"What can we do to help?" Trent called as he approached Mrs. Gunnerson.

"Find my boys!" she answered. "They was downriver runnin' some cows out o' this cornfield."

"Oh, Lord," Willie muttered, urging his horse into a gallop. Trent followed, and the two of them eased past men fighting the fire and rode on. They circled the scorched cornfield and trotted on to the river. Near a clump of towering white oaks, they found what they were looking for.

Willie froze, but Jack Trent rode a few paces farther, then climbed down from his horse. The doctor stepped toward the oaks, drew out a knife and reached up to cut the rope wrapped around Tom Gunnerson's seventeen-year-old neck. After easing Tom to the ground, Trent likewise cut down the smaller figure of Erik Gunnerson. The bodies were stripped naked, and the ugly black letters SCAR were burned into their rumps with a branding iron.

"What sort of man does a thing like that?" Trent demanded to know. "God in heaven, is such cruelty possible?"

Willie finally managed to slide off his saddle. He took a blanket from his horse and carried it to where the doctor had laid the Gunnerson brothers side by side.

Trent shuddered as he unfurled the blanket over the corpses. "Boy was barely fourteen. Not much older than Billy. Wasn't branding them enough, Wil? Did they have to hang them, too? And to leave them like that!"

"Was to make a point," Willie said, grinding his teeth. "Put these farmers on the run."

"Won't work," a young voice announced from the trees.

Willie turned in surprise as the other young Gunnersons, twelve-year-old Matthaus and ten-year-old Stefan, emerged from cover.

"You saw it all?" Trent asked.

Stefan nodded as he collapsed against the doctor's side.

"Tom sent us to cover," Matthaus explained. "Erik was to go, too, but he wouldn't. I should have stayed."

"No, Erik should have hidden," Willie argued. "Tom, too."

"We're on our own land!" Matthaus screamed.

"And now we've got to bury your brothers here," Willie told them.

"We're in the right," the boy argued as tears flowed down his face.

"Right's got nothin' to do with it," Willie countered. "We're talkin' about livin' and dyin'."

"Yes, it is," Grandma Gunnerson shouted as she rode her mule across the scorched earth. "I buried these boys' papa and two boys besides hereabouts, the three of 'em dropped by Comanche arrows. Matthaus, where's Tom got to? And Erik."

"Ma'am, you best prepare yourself for bad news," Willie advised.

"Both of them?" she asked, noticing the blanket. Trent nodded, and she stepped down from the mule with only a slight quiver.

"Grandma, don't," Matthaus said, stepping between the old woman and the corpses.

"My boys were scalped and cut up fearful," she said, pulling Matthaus aside. "Do you think any man alive can do worse? I've got a nose, and I can see. Wasn't hams they hung from them ropes, Doc, and there's been flesh burned as well."

"Show her, Jack," Willie said, drawing little Matthaus back.

Trent slid the blanket back from the waxen faces, but

Mrs. Gunnerson insisted on seeing the worst. She stifled a cry and glared across the river where the Scarlet ranch began.

"There's been many a child buried here," she began, "dead of snakebite and sickness, hunger and heartache. Arrows and bullets have taken their share. But never has murder been signed!"

"Those brands go a long way toward provin' it's Scarlets at work, ma'am, but a jury will want more," Willie warned.

"More'n what?" Matthaus cried. "Stef and I saw 'em do it. Was Jim Scarlet put the ropes around their necks, and it was Scarlet horses the other men rode. I don't know all the names, but I remember the faces just fine. We won't let Tom and Erik be the only ones to hang."

"Send for Wade Maddock," Trent advised.

"Been done already," Grandma Gunnerson announced as she drew her surviving grandsons close. "I'd deem it a special kindness, Doc, if you could bring Tom and Erik along home. It's proper they rest with their pa and ma and uncles. You and Mr. Fletcher can swear to seein' them brands. No need anybody else should look at 'em that way."

"No, ma'am," Willie said. "We'll see it's done."

CHAPTER 13

Willie accompanied Jack Trent to the Gunnerson farm-house, but he didn't linger. There were plenty of hands available to dig graves, and Willie felt like an uninvited guest. Kin and neighbors sobbed as they recalled better times. Willie felt only cold and hollow. He'd only met the Gunnerson boys once, and he owned no memories of yellow-haired renegades racing plow horses, of shy young-sters taking their first steps or joining in a harvest dance. So it was that when Marshal Wade Maddock called for a posse to pursue the murderers, Willie climbed atop his anxious horse and rode along.

In all, there were ten of them in that posse. Besides Willie and the marshal, eight farmers rested shotguns across their knees and mounted mules or plow horses. Maddock led the way to the river, where the ropes dangling from the white oak marked the death scene.

"Hard to pick up a trail in the river," the marshal grum-bled as he collected the discarded nooses. Willie picked up the abandoned garments torn from Tom and Erik, but Char-lie Dowe snatched them away.

"Better such things are left to friends," the farmer said,

114

glaring at Willie. "We all know who you are, mister. Doc Trent may trust you, but we got out own views."

"Maybe you can find the men who did this then," Willie replied as he stepped to his horse. "You see a trail, Marshal?"

"Where?" Maddock asked. "Tracks lead straight to the river."

"For a time," Willie admitted, "but there's only two good trails back to Scarlet's place, and one of 'em's a quarter mile from here. You men do what you want. I'm headin' that way."

"Marshal?" Dowe asked.

"It could be a trap," one of the others warned.

"You get a look at them boys?" Maddock asked as he climbed atop his horse. "Fletcher there did. Read his eyes and tell me he's leadin' you into a trap. There's pure murder on that man's face!"

Willie heard Maddock's horse splash into the river and others followed as well. It didn't matter. Willie'd made up his mind to find Jim Scarlet whether the rest of them came or not. In truth, he welcomed Maddock. As for the others, they wouldn't amount to much help in a fight.

Willie had no difficulty picking up the tracks of four riders on the north bank of the river.

"It's as you said," Maddock observed. "They'd be the ones. I noticed a track back yonder with a notched shoe, and here it is again."

"That's enough proof to hang 'em," Dowe declared. "More'n they had on my boy Cory."

"There'll be more," Willie told them. "Witnesses. Marshal, you want these four dead or held for trial? Make your mind up, because if we go in shootin', it's best to kill the whole bunch."

"Let's go slow," Maddock urged. "If we take 'em alive, we're sure to find out more about who's back of it all."

"Don't we all know that now?" Dowe cried.

"It's a different thing provin' it," the marshal cautioned. "Fletcher, how would you go about it?"

"Scout ahead and then circle around, cut 'em off from the house. You'll have a war on your hands if Jim Scarlet gets to his brothers, and we're no army."

"He's right," Maddock told the others. "We're goin' ahead. Once we figure things, we'll bring you others along. Meanwhile you ride along slow. Stay a hundred yards or so behind. And watch you don't get surprised from the rear."

The farmers nodded and hung back as promised. Willie and the marshal then rode on.

Willie didn't figure the killers to worry much about pursuit, but he never expected them to stop shy of the Scarlet house. To his surprise Jim Scarlet had made camp a half mile up the trail. The four horses were tied off on one side, and Jim sat beside a small fire roasting strips of beef. His boots were kicked off to one side, and he'd discarded his shirt.

"Looks to be settlin' in for the evenin'," Maddock whispered. "There's one of the others yonder fetchin' water from the spring."

Willie nodded, then pointed to a third man squatting behind a clump of brush. Another figure moved behind the horses.

"I'll bring along the others," Maddock explained. "Get your horse to cover and cut 'em off from their mounts."

Willie nodded. After hiding the gray on the far slope of a nearby hill, he drew his Colt from its holster and cautiously crept toward the killers' camp. Two men Willie didn't recognize joined Jim Scarlet at the fire. One had a jug of corn liquor, and the three of them took turns gulping the alcohol.

"Bet them farmers'll waste no time headin' north now," Jim boasted between swigs.

"Nice touch, brandin' em like that," a shaggy-haired companion declared. "Lord, that little one did squirm. Good thing you gagged him, or he'd raised the dead."

"Wasn't the dead worried me," Jim said, laughing. "Didn't much want anything alive happenin' along."

"Well, ain't anything alive left danglin' from them oaks," the third man claimed. "I make a noose, it works fast. And permanent. Not even much kickin'."

"Big one kicked some," Jim muttered. "Little one snapped his neck like a twig."

Willie felt a fire rage within him as they went on drinking and laughing. He was half prepared to cock his pistol and charge the three of them. Then the fourth figure returned from the horses. Pale as moonlight and stumbling along, Thad Scarlet looked even younger than before.

"Gone and lost your dinner, have you, boy?" Jim jeered. "And here you didn't even join in with the fun."

"Fun?" Thad growled. "One o' them wasn't as big as me. You didn't have to hang 'em, Jim. They was scairt silly, and they'd've left their place fast enough."

"Couldn't have witnesses swearin' out complaints like them Hamer kids," Jim argued. "Besides, they'd not likely showed their bare rumps off. Most folks wouldn't even see our handiwork. This way the fire's drawn a crowd, and the whole batch o' them Yank farmers'll scatter."

"They'll know who did it," Thad complained. "Nobody but us runs that SCAR brand."

"Knowin's just fine," Jim replied. "Provin's another thing."

The others laughed their agreement. Thad collapsed beside his brother and rubbed his eyes. Then Wade Maddock appeared on the road.

"Hold real still, friends," the marshal warned. "I got some men with me less than friendly."

"Run!" the shaggy man screamed as he tossed the jug aside and leaped to his feet. He got three steps before a shotgun blast from the woods threw him to the ground. The second stranger headed for the horses. Maddock fired at him and missed. Willie waited a second longer, then shot him just under the left eye. The killer flayed his arms and

117

dropped to his knees. Then, after muttering a curse, he fell facedown, dead.

"Get those hands up!" Maddock hollered.

Jim Scarlet rose slowly, then swung Thad around between him and the lawman.

"This here's my baby brother!" Scarlet pleaded. "Just a kid. Don't go shootin' anymore. We done nothin'."

"Jim?" the shaggy killer called in dismay. Charlie Dowe stepped over and blasted the top of the man's head off with a shotgun.

"Now for you two," Dowe said as he broke open the shotgun and dropped the spent shells onto the ground.

"That's enough, Dowe!" Maddock yelled.

"Dowe?" Thad asked, his eyes filling with terror. "Jim?"

"That you, Marshal?" Jim asked as he discarded his gun belt. "Lord, what brings the law here? You gone crazy, shootin' up our camp?"

"Come after a pack of cowards," Maddock explained. "Men that like to stick hot irons onto little boys and then hang 'em. Men like you, Scarlet!"

"They was stealin' our cows," Thad mumbled. "Tell 'em how you saw it, Jim. Tell 'em . . ."

"Shut your fool mouth, boy!" Jim barked, slapping Thad to the ground. "Want to put a rope around our necks?"

"You've done that already," Willie said, plucking a branding iron from amid the saddles stacked near the horses. "Smells of flesh. Lord, you didn't even clean it, Scarlet! If this doesn't do it, what I heard you say would."

"We should've let them rustlers do for you on the trail," Jim muttered.

"I don't believe your memory's too fine," Willie said as he marched toward the fire. "It was me should've let them tend to you Scarlets."

"Not me, Major," Thad said, gazing up into Willie's fiery eyes. "I didn't have a hand in this. I swear it!"

"Hush!" Jim shouted as he kicked his brother. Willie

118

reached out and grabbed Jim by the shirt. With a single furious motion, Willie dragged the killer past the fire and slung him against a live oak.

"You touch that boy again, and I'll leave you to these farmers!" Willie warned. "That iron's still handy, you know."

For the first time Jim Scarlet's face lost its color, and he shrank from the encircling farmers.

"Brand him!" Dowe shouted.

"Hang him!" the others added. "An eye for an eye, the Good Book says!"

"These two are my prisoners," Maddock insisted as he cut a length of rope and stepped to Jim's side. The elder Scarlet sat helplessly as the marshal bound his wrists and feet.

"He's yours to do as you will," Willie said, moving over beside Thad and steadying the shivering boy. "But I didn't fish this boy out of the Pease River for anybody to hang. What was your part in all this, Thad? Tell us quick, boy."

"All I did was water the horses," Thad claimed. "I don't hold with what got done."

"If he testifies to that, he's sure to earn mercy," Maddock observed.

"And make sure yon brother's neck's stretched," Dowe added.

"I won't speak against my kin," Thad said, dusting himself off. "You hang me if you want. Like Mr. Fletcher here says, I close to drown last summer, so I got two months more'n I ought to as things stand."

"A judge and a jury'll decide all that," Maddock announced as he readied a rope for Thad's hands.

"No, we will here and now," Willie argued.

"It's not your choice!" Dowe shouted.

"No, I figure it's yours, Mr. Dowe," Willie answered. "You lost a boy not much bigger'n Thad here. As did Miz Gunnerson. Right or wrong, I figure a boy's due another chance. If I'd been doin' the decidin', I'd seen it done that way. We could hang a hundred Thad Scarlets, and you wouldn't be any less sorry to've lost Cory. Nor would it dry any o' Miz Gunnerson's tears. I say leave this boy to get taller . . . and smarter.''

"Charlie?" one of the others asked.

"Marshal, leave that boy to go," Dowe said. "Fletcher's right. Only see here, boy. You got to promise us to walk the straight and narrow. Ain't likely mercy pays a second call on you."

"I never held with what was done this time," Thad said solemnly. "You can know I wouldn't do a thing like that ever, nor especially now."

"Get out of here," Willie said, and Thad scrambled to the horses, threw a blanket and saddle atop one, and headed home. Maddock tied Jim Scarlet atop a horse and left the farmers to likewise bring along the corpses.

"You comin', Fletcher?" Maddock called.

"I had enough o' this business," Willie replied. "I'll be at the Trent place if you need me."

CHAPTER 14

With Jim Scarlett jailed and harvest in full swing, things should have quieted down around Esperanza. They didn't. Bob Scarlet had no intention of abandoning his brother to a hangman nor of permitting the hated farmers to sense a victory either. By night riders paid visits to the very men sure to be called as jurors, and by day Bob himself toured Esperanza, expressing his regrets over the tragic deaths of the farm boys and talking of Jim's blighted childhood and the hard times that had stirred a sort of madness in the young man.

Bob Scarlet did more than make promises where the Gunnersons were concerned. Cash was offered as compensation for the burned cornfield and more was promised.

"Wants to buy my land," Grandma Gunnerson grumbled to Jack Trent. "My land! I've buried boys in that soil! Does he think his greenback dollars will erase the memory of my poor tortured grandsons?"

When cash failed, riders came bearing torches. This time the Gunnersons were ready, though, and two cowboys were blown from their horses by shotgun blasts. The one fire actually set was quickly extinguished by a pail of well water.

"Those Scarlet fellows think it's just an old woman and a pair of boys left out here," Grandma proclaimed in town.

"Matthaus and Stefan did their growing up fast down by the river. As for me, a woman who's seen as many winters come and go as I have doesn't figure she's got much left to lose by standin' her ground."

"There's not an inch of slack in her," Ellen remarked to Willie as they loaded a wagon with oak benches crafted for the schoolhouse. "Marshal Maddock says Jim's prepared to name others to save his hide, too. I wouldn't be surprised to learn the Scarlets had packed up and moved on again."

"I would," Willie replied. "I haven't noticed much slack in Bob either. There's a meanness there though."

"Worried?" she asked. Willie nodded and she laughed. "Imagine that! Willie Delamer worrying. Afraid? I can't recall it ever happening. All those weeks in Edwards, with half-a-dozen men doing their best to kill you, all I saw was poise, confidence. It was like when we were little, riding out past the river. You never once showed a trace of caution. You'd climb those fool cliffs when you knew the rocks were full of rattlesnakes or run your horse across that broken country when a prairie-dog hole might have brought on a killing fall."

"You're wrong about Edwards," he told her. "And other times, before and after."

"You were afraid for us, not yourself," she argued. "You? I don't think death much concerns you."

"Maybe not dying," he admitted. "Been close to that too many times. I figure it might offer some sort of peace. It's the killin' scares me. And it's creepin' up on us fast, Ellie. I can smell it comin'."

When they reached Esperanza, Willie discovered just how close it had come. Dewey Hamer trotted over to help unload the benches. His tanned face had grown pale, and his eyes betrayed concern.

"What's happened?" Willie asked after Ellen stepped inside the schoolhouse.

"Somebody rode in last night and shot Jim Scarlet," Dewey explained.

122

"Know who?" Willie asked.

"Nobody's sure. Marshal Maddock got called out o' town by some cowboys who claimed rustlers got some o' their stock. Wasn't half an hour later Jim got himself shot. Weren't any rustlers. Marshal says it was Bob likely behind it 'cause Jim was goin' to talk at his trial. But word is the Scarlets'll be comin' in to fetch Jim today—and maybe get themselves some revenge."

"Might be best for you to pass the time at your farm then," Willie advised.

"No, Miz Gunnerson sent Matt out to invite people to town. She figures there'll be less trouble if a crowd's here."

"Could be right," Willie admitted. "Or it could be the Scarlets'll have more targets."

Willie concluded the discussion at that point. He dragged the last of the benches inside the school and told Ellen to return home.

"Why?" she asked, and Willie explained. "If there's trouble," she argued, "it's better I stay. Jack's here, and . . ."

"The children aren't. Plan on Billy holdin' off raiders? They could come, Ellie, and the both of us know it."

"You could go," she suggested.

"Will, if that's how you want it."

"They'd be less likely to harm a woman, I suppose," she said, frowning. "And if they want a fight, I can still hit what I shoot at. Stay here and watch out for Jack. He speaks up far more than is altogether safe."

"Can't hold back the truth, Ellie."

"A man that's got little children hasn't always got the right to speak out," she complained. "It's brought on trouble before, remember? And I worry it will again."

"Could be," Willie agreed. "I'll keep an eye on him."

Willie passed the next hour sitting on the porch of Rupert Hamer's store. For a time Dewey wandered over and spoke of hunting deer along Salt Fork, but Willie was distracted

123

and merely nodded at the boy's words. Dewey had gone back inside the store when young Thad Scarlet rode into town alongside his brother Webb. They brought with them a barebacked mare.

"We come to take our brother home," Webb announced when Wade Maddock stepped out to greet them.

"You didn't waste much time in gettin' here," Maddock observed. "Only sent a man to tell you a bit ago."

"Word travels fast," Webb explained as he dismounted. The marshal nodded to a pair of farmers, and the men stepped inside the jailhouse and brought Jim Scarlet out. The corpse was wrapped in a heavy wool blanket. Webb paused only long enough to take a glance beneath the blanket and satisfy himself it was really Jim.

"Lay him 'cross yon horse," Webb ordered, and the farmers did just that.

"Sad day for law when a prisoner's shot down in jail," Marshal Maddock announced in a voice loud enough for all to hear. "Strange how it happened. Must've been a familiar face, as ole Jim was right up next to the window when they shot him. If he'd tried to hide, the walls would've protected him."

"Not if he was kilt from the inside," Webb grumbled.

"He wasn't," Maddock assured the younger Scarlets. "There were casings outside the window. Whoever it was used a new Remington revolver. Expensive gun, not the kind one o' these farmers'd own."

"Meanin'?" Webb asked.

"Not sure what as of yet," the marshal answered. "But I expect to find the pistol that did this work, and I'll hang the man that's carryin' it. What kind of pistol's that you're carryin', Webb?"

A look of pure hatred flowed across Webb Scarlet's face as he shrank from the marshal's question.

"Want to see mine?" Thad asked, drawing a shiny new Remington from its holster. "Figure I snuck in here and kilt my own brother, Marshal?"

"I don't figure to know . . . yet," Maddock replied. "But I will. It's time an end was put to this fight. There's been enough killin'."

"Enough?" Webb called, laughing. "Why I figure it's only just begun, Marshal!"

"Do you?" Maddock cried. "Who's to be next, Webb? You? Maybe your little brother here?"

"He ain't so little he can't shoot farmers," Webb retorted. "Or marshals, either one. Don't go pressin' your luck, Maddock. I remember when you was only a broke-down saddle tramp lookin' for whiskey money down in Albany. Don't think that star'll promise you a long life."

"That a threat, sonny?"

"Just friendly advice," Webb insisted. "Now you go sit in your jail and try to figure out which skunk of a farmer shot my brother. 'Cause if you don't, I will."

Thad hopped down and helped Webb tie Jim's stiff body across the roan's back. When that was done, the two Scarlets mounted their horses and turned toward home. Thad led the mare along as they went.

"They'll be back, won't they?" Dewey asked from the doorway.

"Sure, and then it'll be somebody else's turn to wrap a body in a blanket," Willie declared. "Dewey, you be cautious ridin' to and from town, hear me?"

"We got our corn in, Major," the boy explained. "I'll be stayin' with Uncle Rupe for a time."

"Then keep your head down, son," Willie advised. "It's what I plan to do."

It proved to be good advice. In the week that followed, two farmhouses were burned, and old Abner Settles was killed on his way into town for supplies.

"Bob Scarlet bought out Grandma Settles," Ellen explained at breakfast the next day. "Paid five hundred dollars for a farm worth five times that."

"Was a mistake to sell," Trent grumbled.

"She's got the grandchildren to worry about," Ellen said, sighing. "Little Oscar came to school in tears. Some riders chased him from the road. Then Grandma Settles found her door burned with the SCAR brand. Nobody's forgotten what happened to Tom and Erik Gunnerson."

"It's time we had a gathering, decided what to do," Trent declared. "I'll speak to Granny Gunnerson and the marshal."

"You watch who's nearby when you do," Willie warned. "Been a lot of strangers around Esperanza the past few times I've ridden through there. You know Ted Slocum's offered to send some men up here to help watch the farm."

"Cowboys?" Ellen asked. "They'd hardly be welcome."

"They would be in a fight!" Willie barked. "And it'll come to that unless Bob Scarlet gets rid of everybody with a few fires and some night shootin'."

"These people don't know what to do," Trent explained. "And we don't know all this is Scarlet's doing."

"We don't?" Willie asked. "As for these people, they held off Comanches out here a half-dozen years, and they fought the South down to a nub before that."

"He's right, you know, Jack," Ellen told her husband.

"Usually is," the doctor grumbled. "And me, well, I just make mistakes."

Trent stormed out the door, and Ellen hurried after him, leaving Willie to stare at the dumbstruck children.

"He's scared, Uncle Wil," Billy said by way of explanation. "We are, too. Been riders by the school. Mama won't say so, but they've said scary things to her."

The others nodded, and Willie scowled.

He accompanied Ellen and the children into town as usual that morning, but there was no sign of riders. Instead of returning home, Willie lingered in town. He soon found himself searching the face of every man in town, noting which were farmers in buying supplies and which were strangers stopping by Hamer's Store or idling on the street.

"Ain't no law against visitin' a town, is there?" one young man responded when Willie confronted him.

A second bit off a chaw of tobacco and explained his father was over at Hamer's, selling a load of wool.

"Heard you had trouble here," the stranger added. "We had our share o' cowmen down on the Concho. Figure they own all Texas, and they're quick to shoot bullets into anybody that argues."

The only shooting to happen that day occurred an hour after midday. Willie was at Hamer's eating a cold biscuit stuffed with dried beef that Dewey had offered when twin pistol shots shattered the quiet.

"Major?" Dewey cried as he dropped to the floor. Willie pulled his own pistol and hurried to the door. A rider galloped off into the dust, chased by a second pair of pistol shots. Wade Maddock stumbled out into the street, favoring his left leg.

"You see him?" the lawman called to Willie.

"Just the dust," Willie said, holstering his pistol. "He shoot at you?"

"Put a hole in my leg!" Maddock shouted. "Was hidin' behind a barrel. Poor shot not to've kilt me!"

"Wish I'd known," Willie said, shaking his head. "I was in fine shape to notch his skull."

"Wish you had, Fletcher. I ain't high on findin' myself a target."

"Dewey, ride out and fetch the doc," Rupert Hamer shouted as he rushed over to the wounded marshal's side. "Now!"

"Fool thing to do," Maddock muttered as Hamer helped him to the store. "Go and get shot from ambush!"

"You wasn't the first!" Charlie Dowe yelled, leading a half-dozen comrades toward the store. "Deputize us, Marshal. We'll track down that cowboy."

"He's halfway to tomorrow," Maddock argued.

"No, he's gone to Bob Scarlet's place," Dowe asserted. "We all know it. Give us a warrant and leave us to ride out and settle accounts. We'll see justice done."

"Justice?" Maddock cried, wincing as Rupe Hamer tightened a binding around the bloody thigh. "Listen to me. Ain't a one of you got any proof them Scarlets had a hand in this. If you do, speak out, and I'll lead you to the ranch myself. You don't, hold your water."

"We held back long enough!" Dowe shouted, and a chorus of others agreed. The marshal was not to be swayed though.

If Wade Maddock hadn't been shot, Dr. Jackson Trent never would have come to Esperanza that fateful September afternoon. And if Trent hadn't come, Willie likely wouldn't have stayed. Such was the way fate wove its cloth, shaping events with no more rhyme or reason than a chicken pecking at its feed. One minute Trent was in the back room at Hamer's Store, cutting a bullet from Wade Maddock's tough hide. A half-hour later Trent was helping the marshal across the street to the jailhouse when a pair or riders thundered up the road, blasting away with pistols at anything that moved.

"God, no!" Dewey Hamer screamed as he threw himself behind a wagon while bullets tore splinters of wood from the buildings beyond.

Marshal Maddock, game to a fault, hopped away from Trent, drew a pistol, and emptied his gun into the closets of the assassins. For a brief instant the two men exchanged shots and curses. Maddock finally fell facedown into the dusty road, and the rider tumbled from the saddle. The second rider made a dash toward Hamer's Store, but Willie was crouching just inside the door and fired a single shot into the horseman's skull as he raced past.

For half a minute awkward silence froze the street. Then a woman began to wail. There was a rush of frantic feet flying from the schoolhouse and a moan or two from injured onlookers. Dewey Hamer managed to pry himself from the ground and step over beside the marshal.

"Uncle Rupe?" the boy called. "He's all bloody."

"He's dead," Jack Trent called as he dragged himself to the lawman's side.

A crowd of the shocked and curious began to gather. Willie joined them rather belatedly. First he assured himself of his marksmanship. The fleeing rider was, indeed, quite dead. Next Willie had a look at the other killer. Maddock's pistol had torn apart the man's chest. Willie stared at the stupid grin on the young man's face and fought to recall where he'd seen it before.

"He was at the trial in Throckmorton," Dewey whispered. "One of the ones that brought Cory in."

Charlie Dowe stepped over and kicked the corpse hard in the stomach.

"For my boy!" the farmer cried angrily.

"He's past feelin', Mr. Dowe," Dewey said, gripping the old man's hand.

"I ain't!" Dowe exclaimed, kicking the corpse a second time.

Willie started to pull Dowe aside, but the sound of Ellen calling his name tore him away. He rushed past Maddock's body and plunged through the crowd until he located her kneeling beside her husband.

"Looks like I jumped into trouble again," Jack Trent said, gazing up with glassy eyes.

"Willie, he's hurt," Ellen cried.

Willie nodded as he bent down had helped Trent from the ground. The doctor's left arm dangled helplessly at his side, and a fist-sized red circle continued to swell across his middle.

"Take him to the jail," Rupert Hamer suggested. "It's closest."

Willie nodded and started in that direction. Other hands reached out, and soon six of them were carrying Jack Trent to the jail. They laid him on the marshal's desk, and Ellen shooed the others out the door.

"No, Wil, you stay," Trent called as Willie turned toward the door.

129

"Help me bind the wounds," Ellen urged, and Willie started to tear a strip from his shirt.

"Don't waste the time," Trent said, coughing blood. "I've worked on too many bodies not to know which will mend. The arm's just broken. It's the bullet went through the thorax that's sure to kill me. I've only got one lung working, and it won't last long."

"Don't talk nonsense," Ellen growled.

"Hush and fetch the children!" Trent barked. "Now!"

The urgency in his voice sent Ellen reluctantly on her way. Once she was gone Trent grasped Willie's arm and stared intently into his eyes.

"Seems we're forever bringing you into our trouble," the doctor mumbled.

"Didn't know you to hold title to it all," Willie countered.

The doctor shuddered and spit up blood, and Willie turned.

"I'll holler for Ellie," he offered.

"No, it's you I need to talk to," Trent insisted. "Don't have long now, and there are things need saying."

"Not to me," Willie argued.

"Especially to you, Wil. Ellen's never kept her feelings a secret. She never could. We're more than just husband and wife, you know. We're friends."

"No, she and I are friends, Jack. You're . . ."

"Hush and let me finish," Trent said, coughing violently. "I know all about everything. More than you do, I sometimes think. Ellen, the war, your brother . . . but it doesn't any of it matter. What does is Ellen . . . the children. They all love you, and I think you love them, too. I see it in your face. They're going to need you, Wil."

"Not me," Willie argued. "You!"

"That can't be now," the doctor explained. Tears formed in his eyes, and he shuddered. "Promise you'll look after them, take care of them. Promise . . ."

"You know I will," Willie pledged.

130

Trent started to speak, then stopped when he saw Ellen appear in the doorway with the children. Willie instantly withdrew, and Ellen took his place at Jack Trent's side. The boys stood somberly beside their father. Little Anne cried openly, and the boys soon joined in.

"He's bad, isn't he?" Dewey asked when Willie stumbled out the door.

"He's dyin'," Willie answered.

The townfolk gathered outside the jail for half an hour. Some cursed Bob Scarlet. Others prayed. Many wept. Then Ellen led the children out the door and announced her husband was dead.

"We'll see he's tended proper, ma'am," Rupe Hamer promised.

"I want the ones who did this punished!" she yelled in reply.

"They're dead, the both of 'em!" Charlie Dowe explained.

"No, they're not the ones responsible!" Ellen shouted. "We all know who is! Willie?"

"I'll backtrack their horses," he offered.

"Why bother?" Dowe muttered. "Why not get some rope and do what we should've done that day you found the Gunnerson boys down at the river?"

There were shouts of agreement, and a dozen hands volunteered to join a posse.

"Will you lead us, Major?" Dewey asked.

"I got a grave to dig," Willie told them. "Then I'll backtrack their trail. After that, we'll make a plan."

"That's a waste of time," Dowe argued.

"You go now, you'll only get half of you killed," Willie warned. "What's needed ain't reckless courage. It's a plan. Bide your time, and we'll settle accounts without fillin' a graveyard. Hear me?"

They did, and they nodded. But their faces were full of disappointment. And something else—suspicion.

131

CHAPTER 15

There wasn't much to the burying. Ellen tended her husband's body herself, and two of the farmers who were handy with hammers built Jack Trent a coffin of scented red cedar. Willie and Dewey Hamer carved out twin graves from the rocky ground beside the church.

"Maybe it's not a proper graveyard yet," Dewey's Uncle Rupert admitted, "but we'll fence it later and get a real preacher to bless it. It's fittin' the doc and Marshal Maddock should rest in hallowed ground."

Willie recalled a South Carolina colonel remarking any ground touched by the graves of the valiant was hallowed ground. Still, Rupe Hamer and the others meant to honor Trent and the marshal.

As for their killers, Charlie Dowe scooped out a hole behind the jail for them. They had no cedar casket, nor even the patchwork quilt Wade Maddock was wrapped in.

"If not for the women arguin' on it, they'd not been buried at all," Dewey remarked as he passed a spade into Willie's waiting hands. "Mr. Dowe judged 'em buzzard meat."

"Well, I don't suppose you'll find anybody cryin' over 'em."

"Nope," Dewey agreed. "Not around Esperanza, you won't."

That evening close to two hundred people gathered to express their sympathy and to mourn the passing of Throckmorton County's only doctor. Others said prayers over Wade Maddock. There were hugs for the children and offers of help to Ellen. Besides the farm folk, Travis Cobb had ridden out with his whole brood, and the TS outfit was there in force, too.

"It's grievous news," Travis said as Ellen collapsed against his side. "I worried somethin' of the sort would happen. Even with Willie here, they still killed him."

"Wasn't his fault," Ellen declared, turning to face Willie's haunted face. "Jack was just in the line of fire. Wrong place, wrong time. He told me so himself."

"Best you and the little ones come along to the ranch now," Travis suggested. "Be safer there. Less memories, too."

"I've got no bad memories where Jack's concerned," she argued. "Besides, there's the school. My work."

"We need the children to help husk the corn," Grandma Gunnerson said. "Take a week for your grief, Miz Trent."

"My family's known pain and grief aplenty," Ellen explained. "And we're not accustomed to hiding our heads in the ground or crying over what's past. As for the school, keeping busy will be a balm. The children will help mend the tears in my heart."

"There's children at the ranch who'd welcome a school," Ted Slocum spoke up.

"Was ranch people kilt her man!" Charlie Dowe barked. "Ain't no forgettin' that, mister! We'll look after her just fine."

"That's not your place, Dowe," Travis objected. "She's my sister. My blood!"

Dowe muttered angrily, then took a wild swing at Travis. The rancher danced out of the way, then blocked a second punch.

"Old man, I come to bury my sister's husband, not bloody a fool farmer," Travis growled.

"Please, he's right," Willie said, pulling a red-faced Travis away from the fuming Dowe. "Ain't the time nor the place."

"What do you know about anything!" Dowe shouted. "Fletcher, he calls himself. Ain't his real name, you know. He's used others here and there. I heard he used to hire himself out to ranchers up in Colorado, and in the Cimarron country, too. Shootin' farm kids was a special talent up that way. And in Kansas . . ."

"Mr. Dowe, that's enough," Ellen cried. "You're hurt because your boy was hung, and I feel for you. But that wasn't Willie's doing, nor was it mine. This is a day for prayer and meditation, for healing. But I swear, if you don't clam up, I'll close your fool mouth myself!"

Dowe shrank from her words, and the crowd hushed.

"Friends, let's have no bickering," Ellen pleaded. "Jack wouldn't have wanted discord. Let's celebrate God's word and remember these two very good men. Then enjoy this good food brought by our thoughtful neighbors. If you have to spit angry words at each other, won't you please do it elsewhere!"

There was a murmur of approval from the other women, and an "amen" or two shouted by the men. The crowd quieted long enough for old Mrs. Gunnerson to offer up a prayer. Others among the crowd remembered kindnesses extended by Dr. Trent or Marshal Maddock. Finally the dead were lowered into their graves, and the holes were filled in with dirt and rock.

"We'll be missing you, Papa," Billy Trent whispered as he sprinkled pebbles atop the mound of earth that marked his father's resting place.

"Won't ever be the same," Ellis added.

"Not ever," Cobb agreed.

Little Anne just whispered her father's name and knelt beside the stone marker not yet inscribed with Jack Trent's name.

"Trav's right, you know," Willie told Ellen as they gazed sadly at the solemn children.

"To his way of thinking," Ellen agreed. "Nobody's out to do us harm, though, Willie. Jack was nobody's enemy."

"He did his share of speakin' out, Ellie."

"He was no threat, and neither am I," she objected. "I want this school to succeed. It can be a sort of legacy for Jack. And I want to raise his children on Salt Fork, where he brought us."

"This ain't over, Ellie," he pointed out. "No, it's barely even begun. I've buried too much of the good things I've known. I won't bury them," he added, nodding toward the children. "Nor you, either."

"I haven't asked you to, have I?"

"You won't reconsider?"

"Ever know me to change my mind?" she asked. "Will you come home with us?"

"And do what? Be your guard? If there's no danger, you won't need . . ."

"I need you!" she exclaimed. "And so will they!"

Willie nodded. Then he left her to the comfort of family and friends.

He was sitting on a low hill a hundred yards east of the schoolhouse when Dewey Hamer appeared with a spare plate of food.

"Figured you might be hungry," the young man declared as he set his extra plate beside Willie and began emptying the one in his hands. "Got some good ham here, honey-cured by Granny Gunnerson. There's good greens and some stewed carrots. Be peach pie later if you want some."

"Not hungry," Willie growled.

"Can't go blamin' yourself, Major. Nobody could've known."

"I should have," Willie grumbled. "It's why I came to town. Why can't I just once have done a thing right?"

"That's what I ask myself sometimes," Dewey confessed. "Don't seem a lot to ask, so Ma says. Just do a thing right now and then. But mostly I make a mess of the important things."

"You ain't full-grown, Dewey."

"How old were you when you went to war? Yeah, I know all about that from talkin' to Mike Cobb. I'm fifteen myself, you know. Older'n Erik Gunnerson's ever goin' to be."

"True," Willie said, sighing.

"So you see you ain't the only one's lost a friend. And broodin' won't heal the hurt."

"What will?" Willie asked.

"Nothin', not really. But I thought maybe some food'll help. And after, I got the rest o' the day off from chores. Maybe we can do some trackin'."

"This won't be any ride to the river," Willie warned.

"I got a rifle tied back o' my saddle, Major. Ain't altogether a bad shot."

Willie recognized in the boy's sad eyes something of himself. He knew pain and loss had brought early wisdom to Dewey Hamer. Willie chewed a square of ham and found it as delicious as the boy had promised. And afterward he and Dewey took a try at tracing the killers' path.

It was a waste, of course. Too many horses had churned the dusty road, and the ground near the river proved too rocky to hold tracks anyway. Even so, Willie suspected the trail led to Bob Scarlet. But suspicions weren't worth much when set on the scales of justice.

Oh, the sheriff did come up from Throckmorton to hear the tale, and he sent a deputy named Eli Carpenter by now and then to look after Esperanza. Carpenter had a boyish face and an easy manner, and folks soon discovered he wasn't nearly so interested in spying trouble as avoiding it. He danced around Bob Scarlet entirely, and aside from passing out county tax bills in October, Eli Carpenter might as well have passed his hours on the face of the moon.

Fortunately the farmers were busy getting crops to market, and for once the Scarlets laid low. Still, an occasional cow strayed into a field, and once a band of drunken cowboys bothered the Marcy girls. But rifles remained silent, and the only blood to flow came from skinned knees or scraped elbows.

Willie stayed, as promised, at the Salt Fork, looking after things in Jack Trent's absence. He didn't enjoy the hard stares of neighbors or the whispers he knew were uttered behind his back. For himself he didn't care what they called him. He resented the barbs sent Ellen's way, though, and the jokes spread around the schoolyard for Billy to hear.

He took out his anger at the woodpile, splitting oak logs as another might have halved twigs. And he passed the time working his horses and erecting a low stone wall enclosing the house and barn.

"Making us a fort, Uncle Wil?" Billy asked finally.

"Of a sort," Willie confessed. "Out here on the edge of things, it doesn't hurt to have a wall or two between you and what's beyond."

"You think maybe the men that shot Papa'll come here?" Billy asked nervously.

"No, they're dead," Willie assured the youngster.

"I miss Papa, you know," Billy said, stepping over as Willie rested his ax against the woodpile. "Especially at night."

"Oh?"

"He used to tell us stories. And when he thought we were asleep, he'd come in and draw our blankets up against our chins."

"In the summer?" Willie asked, grinning.

"No, when it turned cold, like now," Billy said, cracking a grin. "Ma does it sometimes, but not every night."

"She has a lot to worry after, Billy."

"You could do it, Uncle Wil."

"I'm not your papa, Billy."

"No, but he told me if I was to start missing him, I should go talk to you."

"When did he say that?" Willie asked.

"When he was in the jail. You know. Dying."

"Be a tall order for me to do for you what he did, Billy. Jack Trent was as fine a man as I ever knew. And a better one than me by a far sight."

"You're not so bad," Billy said, leaning against Willie's sweaty side. "And you're here."

Willie rested a hand on the ten-year-old's shoulder and felt a shudder run through the youngster's body. Billy glanced up, forced a grin, then dashed off past the woodpile. Willie could still hear the boy weeping half an hour later.

Willie did his best by the children, and he offered what comfort he could to Ellen. Each night thereafter he shared some story, and from time to time he'd even look in on the little room the three boys shared. Most times Billy cracked open an eye and nodded with approval. Cobb and Ellis were usually dozing, though their feet and hands often flayed at the air, and they muffled nightmare cries when their dreams turned dark.

Little Anne slept with Ellen. Not so long before the girl had been a magpie of chatter, but mostly Anne now gazed fearfully at strangers and shrank from the slightest sound.

"It's just the tree frogs," Willie said when Anne clung to his side one night.

"They might bite me," Anne whispered fearfully.

"No, they like little girls," Willie assured her. He spun for her a tale of a handsome prince transformed into a toad by a spiteful witch.

"I always knew you had gifts, Willie," Ellen told him afterward when they sat together on the porch gazing at the autumn moon. "She'll sleep sound tonight, though you may find her chasing after toads to kiss tomorrow."

"That could be a problem," Willie admitted, grinning.

"To be truthful, I'll welcome the sound of running feet. Or any other sound. It's so deathly quiet now that Jack's gone."

138

"Sure, it always gets that way once summer's gone."

"I miss him so much, Willie."

"It's only natural, what with all the years you shared. And the little ones."

"Do you think he knew I loved him, Willie?"

"That's a strange question to send my way, don't you think?"

"It's one I could never answer for myself. He knew he wasn't my first love. I never hid my feelings. When we met, I was still mourning you. I don't suppose I'll ever completely forgive you or Trav, either one, for that lie. Part of me died the day he told me. So many dreams . . . And then Jack came along. I'd taken sick, along with half the county, and Jack came down from Decatur to treat us. He was such a gentle, good man. He didn't hurry me like some had. I felt I owed him my life, and with you dead . . ."

"I was glad to hear you married," Willie lied. "To know something would live on from all those fine dreams we'd shared back on the Brazos."

"We'll never know what might have been had you come back, of course. But I never would have married Jack if you had. And there never would have been a Billy or Cobb or Ellis or little Anne."

"Seein' them's been a comfort, Ellie. Oh, it tore at me to see so much of you in Billy's face that day up in Edwards when I first saw him. And to know he might've been my son if the cards had fallen different. He's a finer boy than I'd likely grown, though, and these past ten years those who rode at my side for long mostly found death there."

"You might have taken a different trail, though, Willie."

"But I'd never been as good a man as the one you took for a husband."

"He *was* a good man, Willie, and a wonderful father. He just wasn't hard enough for life out here."

"He did all right."

"For a time," she muttered. "And then this rock-hard country killed him."

139

CHAPTER 16

Peace proved to be as evasive as ever, and Willie wasn't any too surprised when a party of farmers led by Charlie Dowe appeared with news of more trouble.

"Seems our friend Scarlet's started visitin' folks again," Dowe announced. "First with his piddlin' offers. Then with fire. And if that don't work, he does a bit o' shootin'."

"And where's this happened?" Willie demanded.

"Up and down the river," Dowe answered. "Startin' with old people and workin' 'round to everybody else. Surprised you ain't had visitors yourself."

Twenty eyes stared down at Willie, and he felt uneasy.

"That supposed to mean anything particular?" he asked.

"Means you best call out loud and clear if you cross anybody's land, mister!" a tall farmer named Nichols advised. "Ain't seen you to plow any fields. So far's that's concerned, I don't know we hold with givin' this fine place over to Miz Trent, what with her husband gone and us in need of a doc again."

"He didn't exactly ride off on the noon stage!" Willie shouted. "Don't you figure he paid any price was due on this property?"

"That'll be discussed later," Dowe said, waving his

140

companions down the road toward the river. "You might be wantin' to sit in on the meetin' we're havin' at the schoolhouse after the kids get finished with their lessons. Be discussin' lots o' things. Even you."

Willie turned away angrily, but he took only three steps when Ellen slipped out the front door and halted him.

"It's time we had a meeting," she said. "And it sounds like you ought to be there, Willie. With Jack gone, somebody's got to speak sense."

"You figure there's a man hereabouts who'd listen?" Willie asked, pointing toward the riders speeding north.

"I counted ten of them, Willie. There are sixty or seventy families living north of Esperanza, and some others south. We've got good friends among these people."

"We have?" Willie asked.

"Grandma Gunnerson hasn't forgotten how you brought Matt and Stef back from the river. And there's the Hamers. That Dewey practically worships you."

"Hasn't had a father since he can remember," Willie mumbled. "Elsewise he'd know better."

"And what about Billy?"

"He's got Cobb blood in him," Willie said, grinning slightly. "Cobbs always have been prone to takin' in strays and hopeless mavericks."

She laughed a moment before hurrying inside to speed the children along. They ate breakfast before dawn and washed even earlier. Still, it was a battle to get the four youngsters in the bed of the wagon so that Ellen could reach the schoolhouse on time.

Willie, as was his custom, escorted them into town. That day he stayed rather than return to the house. Esperanza was full of people, for a traveling tinker was peddling goods, and more than a few folks were discussing the town meeting to be held that afternoon at the schoolhouse.

"Heard about the new trouble, Major?" Dewey Hamer asked when Willie visited the store.

"Only what old man Dowe said when he rode by this

141

mornin'," Willie explained. "Scarlet's boys been around, he said."

"Webb was in town yesterday," Dewey said, gazing at his toes. "Boasted by spring there wouldn't be a farmer left in Throckmorton County. Made some threats, and Deputy Carpenter walked over to quiet him down."

"Alone?" Willie asked, tapping his fingers on the pine plank counter.

"Eli was," Dewey explained. "Not Webb. Was witnesses said Eli drew his pistol, but I never knew Eli to wear a handgun. He carried a rifle back of his saddle, and there's a shotgun in the jail. Anyway there were two pistol shots, and Eli falls back into the street dead."

"Does the sheriff know?" Willie asked.

"From what I heard the sheriff lit out for points unknown, scared out of his skin. Webb Scarlet showed up this mornin' with his badge, sayin' he was the new county sheriff. Ain't legal, 'cause Uncle Rupe rode down to Throckmorton and asked. But there's no sheriff there, either, and the county judge is actin' scairt, too."

"So Dowe's called himself a meeting tonight," Willie mused. "To elect a new sheriff, hire a marshal, or some such."

"Was Granny Gunnerson called the meetin'," Dewey explained. "Mr. Dowe's all for ridin' out and havin' a showdown with them Scarlets right now. I don't figure that'd be too smart, though. Webb had himself two mighty mean-lookin' friends yesterday, and some more besides rode through awhile ago. Guess you know the Kinseys come through on their way to Colorado. Sold their place or what was left of it after the fire."

"Their place is over next to the Trents'," Willie said. Dewey nodded gravely. "Is there somethin' else you haven't told me, Dewey?"

"Only that Miz Kinsey said she didn't dare stay. Didn't want killers on both sides of her. You know, with the Marcys sellin'."

"And the other's me?" Willie asked.

"I figure the Scarlets might've hinted you'd take their side."

"Doesn't make any sense," Willie grumbled. "That ground the Marcys held is mostly rock, with only a little good land. If not for their peach orchard, they'd starve. Can't grow enough corn to pay the taxes. It doesn't have much water, either. It's a poor place to farm, but as for cattle, well, they'd find a hundred gullies to stumble down."

"Got him the Kinsey place, too," Dewey pointed out. "Lot of good land there. Has Ma worried. Her place and Mr. Dowe's land come next, besides Miz Trent's I mean."

"Maybe you ought to pass a bit more time with your ma," Willie observed.

"Or might be she should come into town," Dewey remarked. "Ain't much I can do to stop Webb Scarlet and his hired help."

No, Willie thought, that's for somebody else. Dewey Hamer's eyes made no secret as to whom he expected to tend to the job.

The meeting that afternoon was well attended. Feelings ran high, and there was a lot of angry fist-pounding and a fair portion of cursing. It startled Willie to hear coarse talk, what with women and children present, but tempers were overheated. Three times open warfare erupted with Charlie Dowe being the cause twice.

"Cowards!" he shouted to the others. "Won't even a dozen men step forward to ride with me? We can put an end to those Scarlets once and for all."

"Sit down, Charlie!" Grandma Gunnerson demanded. "Now, are we agreed the first task before us is to hire a marshal? Or sheriff, if the county agrees. It should be a veteran lawman, one who has dealt with this sort of trouble before. Agreed?"

There was a wave of agreement in spite of Dowe's objections.

143

"That's all well and good, Granny, but who will we get?" Rupert Hamer asked.

"Ellen Trent's brought me a name," Mrs. Gunnerson explained. "In fact, we wired him this morning in hopes you would all agree."

"Who?" the people asked.

"My brother Lester," Ellen explained. "He's a U.S. marshal in Kansas just now, but he's agreed to accept the job."

"Does he have experience?" Hamer asked.

"Plenty, and he's bringing two deputies," Ellen explained. "He figures to hire a third here," she added, turning toward Willie.

"Be good to have somebody on our side," Dowe confessed. "Four men? Ought to even the odds some."

"He won't be just on our side," Ellen argued. "He'll come to enforce the law. He made that clear."

"So far as I can see, the law's side and ours are one and the same," Grandma Gunnerson declared. "And I also figure any man comes to Esperanza with a star on his shirt's certain to be a target for some."

"He'll need our help," Dewey added. "Eyes, ears, and later on guns."

"He'll have mine," a voice called. Another and another pledged support.

In the end, Willie knew, it would be up to Les and his deputies to keep the peace, though. Those farmers could get mad easily enough, but it would take a lot of molding to make soldiers of them. More likely they'd wind up full of bullets.

Lester Cobb arrived from Kansas the third week of October. Red-haired and freckled, Les seemed too young to have served the law ten years in the Colorado and Dakota territories and later in Kansas. He had the hard gaze and steel-blue eyes of a fighter, though. Willie welcomed him eagerly.

"These two fellows I brought along are sure to be a help," Les boasted, nodding to his companions. "Here's Alf Lowell, fresh from two years with the Pinkertons."

Willie shook hands with an eager, barrel-chested young man with long blond hair and a generous mustache.

"Other one there's Joe Eagle," Les went on, pointing to a man in his mid-twenties with the broad face and straight nose characteristic of the Cheyenne.

"Joe," Willie said, offering his hand. The Indian turned away.

"Don't take it hard, Wil," Les said, shaking his head. "He's temperamental, but he can track anything that walks or runs. His folks died with ole Black Kettle on the Washita River. Was raised white by mission folk before runnin' off with some Ute army scouts."

"I've known the Utes," Willie declared. "And rode some with the Cheyennes in the Big Horn country. Good people who've come to a sad end."

"Wil here grew up racin' horses and huntin' buffalo with the Comanches," Les explained. "Sometimes I suspect he ain't got any use for white folk either."

"Yes?" Eagle asked, taking an interest in Willie for the first time.

"Didn't start out this ugly," Willie explained, opening up his shirt to expose a nasty-looking lance scar. "Was fair buff huntin' hereabouts once, but the hiders've run 'em all down. Got some good-lookin' ponies in the barn there. Come look 'em over. You're sure to want to swap me off of one. That bay nag you're on doesn't look up to hard work."

"Ain't," Eagle grumbled. "Lester's no judge of horses."

"He buys what he can for twenty dollars," Les shouted. "And watch Wil here, Joe. He's apt to trade you out o' your pants."

Willie took to Joe Eagle from the first time the Indian climbed atop a pinto bareback and slapped the pony into a

145

gallop. There was an instant bond among the horse lovers, and it was strengthened that night when Eagle entertained the Trent boys with an old Ute tale of mountain demons and brave warriors.

Les's arrival brought a temporary peace to Esperanza and other changes besides. For one thing, Les took up residence in Ellen's house. Joe Eagle and Alf Lowell shared the barn. And Willie, unused to the company, put together a small cabin down by the river.

"We could as easily have added a room to the house," Ellen complained.

"Nonsense," he argued. "Truth is, I ought to go on back to the Llano. It's not too late to chase down a few range ponies. You've got Les and his men to see you into and out of town and more mouths to feed than you can rightly handle."

"The children need you, Willie," she complained. "And I want you near."

"I won't lie and say I don't want that myself," he confessed. "But it'd be better all around if you had some time to mourn proper. Later on, if you're still of like mind, we ought to do some serious talkin'."

"And now?"

"I won't be far," he promised.

He wasn't either. From the cabin he could watch both the river and road, and he visited the house often. Twice when Les was away Willie passed the night there. Most times he was off chasing down horses or else hunting the river bottoms with Dewey Hamer.

Dewey was a fair shot, but his real talent was sniffing out game. Joe Eagle, who came along now and then, suspected the boy had a trace of Cheyenne blood in spite of his white-blond hair and light features.

"I like huntin' and ridin' all right," Dewey confessed, "but I ain't much on runnin' around in the winter half-naked nor eatin' boiled dog either."

"Which tribe runs bare in winter?" Eagle asked. "So far as dog goes, it can be real tasty. Better than army grub, I can tell you."

Eagle wasn't along the November afternoon when Willie and Dewey dropped two big bucks upriver. After field-dressing the meat, they turned homeward.

"Ma's sure to welcome fresh venison," Dewey declared as he galloped ahead.

"Might welcome your company some, too," Willie added. "You've been at the cabin more nights than not lately."

"Sure, but Uncle Sime looks in on Ma."

They topped a low ridge and to their surprise found Joe Eagle riding toward them. Willie called out a greeting, but Eagle frowned his answer and turned with grave eyes toward Dewey.

"I thought maybe you come out this way," Eagle said. "Lester said I should have a look."

"Trouble?" Willie asked, rising in his stirrups. "Not Ellen and the kids?"

"No, they're well," Eagle insisted.

"Then it's Ma," Dewey declared, stiffening. "Ain't it?"

"They came late last night," Eagle explained. "No moon. A good time for huntin'. Or settin' fires."

"They burned the house then," Dewey muttered.

"House and barn," Eagle explained. "There was some shootin'. I guess she made a fight of it."

"Where is she now?" Dewey asked anxiously.

"We buried her this mornin'," Eagle explained.

"Before I . . ."

"You wouldn't have wanted to see her," Eagle declared. "She was inside the house. It burned."

"Lord," Willie muttered.

"She was dead by then," Dewey said, swallowing with difficulty. "I knew Ma. She'd've put up a good fight. They wouldn't get close enough to light the house till she was down. You were right, Major. I should've been there."

"I counted seven horses," Eagle said, reaching out and gripping Dewey's shoulders. "Seven! You would have made no difference. There were too many."

"Why'd they kill her?" Dewey cried, turning to Willie. "Why her?"

"She was alone," Eagle answered. "Easy. They haven't scared anybody lately."

"They haven't scairt anybody now!" Dewey screamed. "So, Major, you comin' with me? I figure to pay Bob Scarlet a call."

"Not now," Eagle argued. "Lester and Alf have gone already. You should make your prayers . . . and your peace. Later maybe we fight."

"Not much later," Dewey growled. "Major?"

"When the odds are in our favor," Willie replied. "Joe, you find a good trail?"

"So far as the river," Eagle said, nodding somberly. "No tracks beyond. They were careful."

"We all know who done it!" Dewey exclaimed.

"It will take proof to make a case in court," Eagle pointed out.

"You gone and got awful civilized, haven't you?" Dewey asked. "I thought Indians were all for blood feuds and swift justice."

"We learn to walk the white man's road," Eagle answered. "When we can. I promise you this much, Dewey. I won't forget your mother's eyes. Those who did this thing'll be repaid in kind. You got my promise on that."

"Mine, too," Willie added.

CHAPTER 17

After visiting Dewey's mother's grave, Willie escorted the boy to his Uncle Simon's place and left him with family. By nightfall Dewey was back at the cabin, though, shaking with fury and plagued by guilt.

"You should've stayed with your cousins," Willie complained. "You won't find any comfort here."

"Ain't comfort I come lookin' for," Dewey answered. "It's forgettin'. I stay with Uncle Sime, all I see's Ma here and Ma there. It's the same in town at the store. And everybody's near as sad as I am."

"I ain't dancin' a jig myself," Willie said, frowning.

"I thought maybe I could help you work those two black mares you ran down last week. I don't know much about horses, but I learn things fast."

"Sure," Willie agreed. "Stay."

"And while I'm here you can teach me to shoot."

"You know how to shoot," Willie observed. "You've got a better eye than I do."

"There's shootin' and there's shootin'," Dewey said, drawing an old Colt from his blanket roll. "Was Pa's. Teach me how to shoot with it. Uncle Sime says Webb Scarlet rode by the day before the fire and threatened Ma. Said a fire might start up in the barn. May not be proof for a court, but it satisfies me. Teach me to shoot that pistol, Major, and I'll give Webb Scarlet all the justice he needs."

"And if I won't?"

"Then I'll lay in ambush and use my rifle. Either way I'll kill him."

"That's a hard road you're startin' down," Willie warned. "You die a little each step you take. Then finally, when you're all cold and hollow inside, you welcome death. But it doesn't come. Only more killin'."

"I don't understand."

"You will if I start you down that road, Dewey. I'd rather you broke both legs."

As it turned out, there wasn't time for Dewey to learn to shoot a pistol or to do much else. Miranda Hamer's death had stirred the farmers to action. Two days afterward the sound of hammers and axes reverberated through the river bottoms as trees fell. They were cut in five-foot lengths and buried in the rocky ground. Grandma Gunnerson herself drove the wagon with the first wire to the river.

"Barbed wire," Charlie Dowe announced when Willie and Dewey road out to investigate the noise.

"Be a fight for sure now," Willie muttered.

"Been a fight goin' on all along," Dewey cried. "Now it'll be a war."

It wasn't much later when Bob Scarlet appeared to have a look at the fences. Grandma Gunnerson had taken pains to choose the nastiest strands she could find. The long, jagged twists of iron would gash and tear at cow, horse, or man.

"That devil wire's sure to kill my stock!" Bob Scarlet shouted as he nudged his horse into the river.

"Won't much worry a corn plant, though," Mrs. Gunnerson observed.

"It won't have a chance," Bob warned. "Won't be here long enough."

"You touch that wire, we'll be puttin' bullets in your gizzard!" Dowe warned in turn.

"Old man, you've lived too long," Bob declared. "Much too long."

The heated talk continued for nearly an hour. Then the Scarlets turned and rode home.

"We'll be back!" Bob shouted before leaving. There wasn't a soul in Throckmorton County that didn't take that for gospel.

Willie had returned to the cabin by midday. He and Dewey were busy working ponies when Les Cobb arrived.

"Heard you were downriver earlier when the Scarlets had words with Granny Gunnerson," Les called. "Anything said you could describe as a threat?"

"Everything," Dewey answered. "They'll tear them fences down, Marshal. Soon as they can."

"That your view, too, Wil?"

"Could be," Willie said, "but they could slip around and bother a farm or two closer to town if they chose. Ridin' down on that wire, with the river between them and it, offers poor chance of success."

"They can't let the wire stay, though," Dewey argued. "It's as good as admittin' they're beaten."

"There's that," Willie confessed. "And Bob's a man to let his pride swagger him into a tight spot. He's got a lot of men with him, Les. His own and some off ranches to the south stirred up by the fences."

"I know," Les said, sighing. "Had word from Trav on it. Wish there was another way to protect these folks than see 'em raise fences. But they've done about everything else."

"Sure," Willie said, sighing. "So what'll you do, Les?"

"Post myself along that fence line. Joe and Alf, too. Meanwhile you'll watch Ellen and the kids, won't you?"

"You know I will," Willie promised.

* * *

If the storm hadn't come, Bob Scarlet might have made his move that very night. But the way it happened, a blue norther swept down from the Rockies a hair after dusk, and everything living found itself a hole to crawl into. Willie was up at the Trent house, prepared to stand watch, when Les and the deputies returned. Already snowflakes swirled in the air, and Willie was glad to turn over his guard duty and head for the warmth of his cabin. There was a fire blazing in the hearth there. No like comforts awaited the deputies in that cold barn.

"You could stay on in the house, Uncle Wil," Billy offered when Willie led his horse from the barn.

"No, you boys snore too much," Willie said, flashing them a grin. "Take in that renegade Indian, why don't you? He tells fair stories, I'm told."

"Not as good as yours," Ellis complained. "You'll come back later?"

"In a day or so," Willie promised. "When the storm breaks."

Snowflakes were but a beginning, though. By midnight a half-foot of white powder covered western Texas, and the temperature dropped past knowing. Even in the cabin, wrapped in heavy buffalo hides and wool blankets, Willie shivered. As for Dewey, the pale boy was nearly frozen.

"Best huddle by the fire," Willie suggested as he pried himself from the hard slat bed. "Won't get much sleep there, but we won't freeze either."

Dewey nodded and crawled back to the hearth. As the snow continued to cascade from the sky, Dewey's teeth chattered a merry tune or two. Willie thanked God for the ample supply of oaks that cluttered those bottoms. The fire blazed hot and bright, and Dewey finally warmed.

"Thought Iowa boys was used to winter," Willie observed when dawn brought the sun back to Texas.

"Thought so, too," Dewey replied. "But then I ain't been from Iowa for a time now."

                              *   *   *

Willie didn't entirely welcome the thaw that followed
two days later. Oh, he was glad of the warmth, true enough,
but he knew once the wind's bite relented, Bob Scarlet
would be on the prowl.

"Watch Ellen for me," Les urged when he took his
deputies back to the fence line. "No moon tonight. He's
sure to come."

Willie nodded his agreement. He and Dewey cleaned
their rifles and readied extra Winchester shells. They had
seen to the care of the horses and were preparing to head for
the Trent house when riders splashed across the river a
hundred yards away.

"Get behind that rock there," Willie said, pointing
Dewey to cover. But before Willie could find his own spot,
a voice called from the river.

"Major? You up there?"

"I'm here," Willie answered. "You eager to test my
aim, are you?"

"No, sir, not at all," a second voice hollered. "Come to
talk. That's all. It's Thad Scarlet. And Randy. We come
alone. Ain't Bob nor anybody else along."

Dewey swung his rifle to bear, but Willie motioned for
him to hold up.

"I count just the two horses," Willie explained. "And I
can't believe those two'd bring me harm."

"They're Scarlets!" Dewey objected.

"They're friends," Willie argued. "Figure the one can-
cels out the other."

So he allowed Thad and Randy to ride almost to the door
of the cabin. The boys dismounted and tied their horses to
a nearby live oak branch.

"So what's brought you out here?" Willie asked as he
led the way inside.

Thad turned to his elder brother, but Randy hesitated.

"Was foolish to come," Thad mumbled. "Can't say
anything."

"About what?" Dewey asked.

"Best you tell me," Willie advised. "And quick. I got to get along to the house."

"Don't," Thad warned. "It's not the place to be this night."

"Oh?" Willie asked.

"Bob's comin' to kill that new marshal," Randy explained. "And the deputies."

"What about the Trents?" Willie asked.

"Them, too," Thad said, shuddering. "And you. Wants this section, and he figures with everybody dead, he can buy it cheap off the county."

"We don't hold with shootin' little ones," Randy declared.

"How 'bout women?" Dewey barked.

"I never took a hand in that, nor did Bob," Randy said, steadying himself. "But it got done all the same. Ain't no steppin' back from it. Bob says we got a fight to the finish. Be no steppin' back from it. Bob says we got a fight to the finish. Be no surrenderin' like durin' the war."

"Why come here?" Willie asked. "Why tell me?"

"I figure to owe you," Thad answered. "Randy, too. You saved us from drownin' at Pease River. Or worse."

"So we're even you figure? And now you can ride down on the Trents without a second thought?"

"Ain't easy, Major," Randy claimed.

"Then don't do it," Willie told them. "Why not stay here with me? I can use more help with the horses. I can see your heart's not in this. If you stick with Bob, you'll both of you find an early grave."

"Ain't any two roads we can travel," Randy said, dropping his chin onto his chest. "Got no choices. A man ain't nothin' if he don't stick to his kin."

"The way Bob's stuck by you?" Willie asked. "Like at Pease River? Or when he puts his strap across your back? Sometimes a brother doesn't deserve much loyalty."

"Sure, but he's still a brother," Thad argued.

154

"And what about the promise you made, Thad?" Willie asked. "This your notion of walkin' the straight and narrow?"

"I tried, Major," Thad said, trembling. "But I'm a Scarlet. If I ain't, then what? You see how it is, don't you, Major?"

"I see you'll be killed," Willie answered. "I won't be hidin', boys. I'll be shootin' bullets at you."

"Then you'll die, too, and what'll be the use?" Randy asked. "Well, we done what we come to do. Squared our debt. Now I guess we'll go find Bob and come get ourselves kilt."

"You'll tell the others, won't you?" Thad asked, growing pale.

"You knew that when you came," Willie replied.

"Been better if you'd left us to drown at Pease River," Thad said. "Or if Dewey there shot us 'fore we got to the cabin." He turned toward his brother and they walked back to their horses.

"Figure it for the truth?" Dewey asked.

"Enough so I want you to ride out to Grandma Gunnerson's place and fetch Les. Tell him exactly what Thad and Randy said, but don't bring everybody. Bob's still apt to make a try for the fences, and seven or eight men behind those stone walls I built could hold off a small army."

"Bob Scarlet's gont one," Dewey pointed out. "Be back with help. Meanwhile, you watch yourself. Be alone up yonder."

"I've been alone before," Willie said, nodding as Dewey threw himself atop one of the black ponies and started toward the Gunnerson farm. "You watch your own hide, Dewey. You're gettin' to be a fair wrangler."

Willie made his way up the hill to the house. After knocking lightly on the door, he waited as Ellen's soft footsteps sped his way.

"Willie?" she whispered when she opened the door.

"Trouble's on the way," he told her. "I don't suppose there's a basement to this place, is there?"

"Don't you know?" she asked. "Of course there's not. How much trouble's coming, and what do we do?"

"Drag out that old shotgun and as many shells for it as you can find."

"I'll fetch Pa's rifle," Billy declared as he stepped out of his room. "Ellis, Cobb, help Mama."

The younger boys hurried after Ellen. A sleepy-eyed Anne stumbled out of the corner bedroom, and Ellen wrapped a fretful hand around the child.

"Safest place to be's the woodpile," Willie said when Billy returned with a long-barreled Winchester rifle. "Those logs'll catch any stray bullets, and the wall behind it offers cover from the back. Ellie, you take the little ones there."

"Isn't room for us all," Billy argued. "I'm comin' with you."

Willie turned and started to scold the boy, but the sight of unkempt blond locks falling across the boy's forehead brought back to Willie his own childhood. Wasn't Willie Delamer always at his father's side? And Billy could fire that rifle. Could be the boy'd be a real help.

Fortunately it didn't come to that. Before the Scarlets arrived, Dewey returned with Les, Joe Eagle, and a handful of well-armed neighbors.

"This time we're ready for the skunks!" Charlie Dowe boasted.

Willie nodded at the confident fury in the old man's eyes. Others, like the former Yank infantry sergeant Jonas Kettle, were more cautious. Youngsters, like Martin Dale and Paul Nichols, were obviously nervous.

"Best you boys stick close to your papas," Willie advised. "Les, you want to take the west wall. I got the east."

"And if they come from the back side?" Eagle asked.

"Guess that'll be for me to watch," Dewey declared as he headed that way. Joe Eagle followed. Willie, meanwhile, crouched behind the rock wall and waited. Billy

Trent huddled at his side, for no manner of persuasion would pry the youngster from his post.

"You get shot, I swear I'll skin you!" Willie muttered.

"Sure you will, Uncle Wil," Billy said, edging closer to Willie's side. "We been missing you, you know."

"Hush," Willie pleaded. "Sound carries a long way in these bottoms."

It did, too, for the Scarlets were still half a mile away when the sound of their horses wading across the river drew Willie's attention. In an instant he brought Dewey and Joe Eagle back from the far walls. The ambush was set. It remained only for the fly to step into the spider's web.

Bob Scarlet led the way personally. His dark, bulky shadow moved ahead of the others. At his side brother Walt trotted along, boasting of the ease with which Bob had brought them up the river and along to the marshal's very door.

"I knew we didn't need to hire anybody this time," Webb muttered as he whipped his horse up beside his brothers. Seconds later the three Scarlets vanished in an avalanche of fire and powder smoke. Someone screamed. A horse leaped over the wall and raced on.

"There's one on the right!" Dowe shouted, and Martin Dale unloaded his shotgun into the chest of Walt Scarlet. The young man, only turned eighteen that summer, shrieked in horror as he stared at the bloody mess below his neck.

"Birdshot!" Dowe grumbled as he turned his own gun on Walt and blasted the boy with twin twelve-gauge barrels. Walt was lifted from his horse and thrown to the ground, a limp mass of torn flesh and broken bones.

Beyond the wall the raiders seemed lost. Rifles and shotguns continued their heavy fire. Then a pair of riders galloped through the gap in the wall, firing this way and that. One shot shattered Jonas Kettle's left elbow. Another smashed Martin Dale's right kneecap and sent the boy crashing to the ground.

"Martin!" Edgar Dale screamed as he rushed to his son's

side. Bob Scarlet got there first. Already hit three times or more, Bob resembled a demon escaped from hell. He swung a pistol across the elder Dale's skull, then fired the same gun directly into young Martin's face.

"Lord!" Willie heard Dewey yell as the bullets tore through Martin's brain.

Bob then slapped his horse into a gallop and escaped southward past the house. A second raider tried the same tactic, but Ellen fired her shotgun at him, and the rider rolled off his horse and coughed out his life beside the woodpile.

No others reached the wall. Perhaps half the raiders managed to turn their horses and retire to the river. The rest died in front of the wall.

Willie and Les counted seven there. Together with Walt and the one Ellen had dropped, it made nine. Charlie Dowe and Edgar Dale, together with the Nicols boy, found two others cowering in the trees.

"We caught a couple of 'em alive!" Paul Nichols called.

"But not for long!" Dale shouted. Two pistol shots followed.

"That was murder," Ellen declared as she huddled with the children.

"Can't much blame him, ma'am," Dewey said. "Marty was just sixteen, you know. Scarlet could've let him be."

Willie didn't find much justification to it, though. He hugged little Billy to his side, and the boy rested his rifle against the wall. It hadn't been fired.

"I'm glad," Willie whispered. "I figure you'll be one to save lives, like your father. Death's got its ways o' findin' folks fast enough without any extra help."

As the powder smoke settled, Les set about collecting the dead. Dewey gathered the horses, and Ellen set up a pair of torches. Thereafter she turned her attention to Jonas Kettle's elbow and Edgar Dale's cracked head. Neither proved particularly serious, and she had both bandaged quickly enough.

Willie stumbled past the wall and had a look at the faces of the dead. He feared finding Thad or Randy there—or perhaps both. They weren't. There was a slight-shouldered boy Dewey recognized as a Diamond H rider, and two of the cowboys were still beardless. Of the others, all but one was recognized as a Scarlet hand. And Dewey recalled him as standing at Webb's side the day Eli Carpenter was shot.

"Well, Marshal?" Dewey asked then. "Figure we've got enough proof for that judge in Throckmorton to issue a warrant?"

"I'll ride down and see him first thing in the mornin'," Les promised. "If our luck holds, we'll be serving papers on Bob tomorrow."

"If we're lucky, he's bled himself to death," Dowe added angrily. "Guess it's time to get Kettle here home. And Martin."

"My poor boy," Edgar Dale lamented as he dropped his face into his hands. "Lord, what'll Alice say?"

"What is there to say?" Ellen asked.

"Lots," Dowe declared. "Pray it's a better place Martin's gone to. And thank the Lord you've got more children. It's what I did when I lost Cory. And it's why Cully's safe at home where these varmits can't get at him."

"Sure," Willie said as he led Billy toward the house. "Children can be a comfort. But there's no place they're really safe if death's got his eye on 'em."

"Uncle Wil?" Billy whispered.

"Just babblin', son," Willie said, squeezing the boy's shoulder. "This's nothin' but a nightmare dream. Be wakin' up from it soon. Won't we, Ellie?"

She helped him up the steps and through the door. From there Billy led the way to the small room now crowded with Les's long bed and the three smaller ones occupied by the boys.

"Take mine," Cobb offered as he stepped off the edge of the bed and opened the blankets for his adopted uncle.

"Go ahead," Ellis agreed. "Cobb and I share lots of times. When we're scared especially."

"Scared now?" Willie asked as he collapsed in the soothing comfort of the cotton mattress.

"Not now you're here," Billy answered.

"Get to sleep, boys," Ellen admonished. "Now."

"Yes, ma'am," Cobb said.

Ellen then drew Anne up onto one shoulder and headed for the back room. Willie smiled as he watched her go. He caught a glimpse of Dewey, too, his powder-blackened face distorted by the fiery light of the torches.

Willie started to beckon Dewey inside, but the youngster had already turned to go.

"He'll be all right," Les announced as he stumbled into the room. "Joe's gone with him. Best you catch some rest, Wil. We're both apt to need it come daybreak."

CHAPTER 18

Willie was still asleep when Les Cobb left for Throckmorton that next morning. Nor did the sound of Joe Eagle and Dewey carving a grave out on the hillside for the fallen raiders rouse him. In fact, Willie didn't wake until nearly noon when a worried Billy Trent finally shook the bed.

"Billy?" Willie asked, blinking his eyes into focus.

"I thought you were dead," Billy explained as he rested a hand on Willie's chest. "You slept so long."

Willie took a glimpse out the window and frowned. It was clearly past morning.

"Too long," Willie said as he threw aside his blanket and searched for his clothes. He couldn't recall undressing. Cobb carried a pair of brown trousers over and Ellis dragged along Willie's boots.

"They're Uncle Les's," Billy explained as Willie stared at the trousers. "Yours are all bloody. Mama's scrubbin' 'em."

"You got blood on your shirt, too," Cobb noted. "We couldn't get that off you, though."

Willie stepped into the britches and then pulled on his boots. The three boys then escorted him to the dinner table.

"Rest well?" Ellen called from the stove.

"Well and long," he answered. "You should've waken me."

"I thought you needed the sleep. That cabin can't offer much comfort," she said as she stirred a pot of venison stew.

"Better'n the barn," Willie replied.

"Mama, you going to ask him?" Billy cried impatiently.

"Ask me what?" Willie said.

"If you would agree to stay," Ellen explained.

"We been thinking about making bunk beds, Uncle Wil," Billy added. "That way there'd be plenty of room. Gets noisy, sure, what with Uncle Les snoring and Ellis talking in his sleep, but the roof keeps out the water, and we stay warm."

"Ellen, people would . . ."

"Les would be there for now," she argued. "And later, well, we've talked of that before. The boys need you here, and so do I. After last night in particular."

"Please," Cobb said, gazing over with imploring eyes. Billy touched Willie's right side, and Ellis wrapped a small arm around one leg. Even little Anne walked over and leaned against him.

"They're right," Les announced as he stepped through the back door. "Anyway, it's time you were settlin' down."

"Maybe," Willie admitted. "But first there's business to tend. Get your warrants?"

"In my pocket," Les explained. "Alf's ridden off to gather a posse. They should be here by the time we empty that stew pot."

"Willie?" Ellen demanded.

"Best settle with Bob Scarlet first," Willie declared.

"That shouldn't take too long, Sis," Les said, grinning at her. "So maybe you boys'll have two uncles to put up with again tonight."

"At least Uncle Wil doesn't snore," Cobb grumbled. "Nor steal my blankets."

"No, just your bed," Les said, lifting the youngster onto

162

one shoulder and pretending anger. The both of them soon broke out laughing, though. It was later, once they'd eaten their fill of stew and hot biscuits, that Les turned solemn.

"I've got seven names on my warrant," Les explained. "Bob, Webb, and five others that've been seen ridin' with them. Likely there are a few more. Two younger brothers, too."

"You didn't name them?" Willie asked.

"Dewey told about their visit, and nobody saw them last night."

They were along, though, Willie told himself. And were certain to be at the house when the posse arrived.

"Speakin' of boys, you aren't bringin' any more kids like that Dale boy, are you?" Willie asked.

"We need numbers, Wil, and there aren't so many eager to go that I can turn down anybody. Dewey'll be along, and he's younger'n Marty Dale was."

"Sure," Willie muttered. "We'll be an army of widows and kids, I suppose."

"No, I ordered Grandma Gunnerson to stay behind and watch the fences."

They shared a momentary laugh. Then Les led the way outside. A dozen riders waited there. Dewey sat atop his fresh-broke black mare between Alf Lowell and Joe Eagle. Charlie Dowe was there, too, together with six stone-faced farmers. This time the youngsters had stayed behind. Aside from Dewey, each face was etched with the hard life years had brought. Dewey's held only pain and anger.

"Best we get at it," Les said, stepping to his horse and pulling himself atop it. Willie's gray was waiting, saddled and ready, so he, too, mounted. Les nodded solemnly, and Joe Eagle led the way toward the river. In half an hour they had ridden the six miles to the Scarlet house.

"Listen up," Les urged as he brought the posse to a halt. "I'm here to serve my warrant, not fight a war. Don't fire unless they start up. But keep yourselves spread wide and close to cover all the same. If they resist, shoot to kill."

"Don't you worry on that account, Marshal," Dowe promised. "We aim to."

Les then waved men to the right and left. When an uneven crescent formed itself, the marshal stepped forward. Willie was on the right with Joe Eagle and Dewey Hamer. Alf Lowell and Charlie Dowe led the left.

There was nothing very menacing about the Scarlet house. Willie half expected to discover an armed camp. Instead two small boys chased each other around a well. Bob's wife sat in a porch swing, cradling a infant on her lap as she rocked to and fro. A small girl played nearby.

"Andrew, Emmett, hurry over," she called to the boys as the posse approached. Meanwhile Webb Scarlet stepped out of the barn.

"What do you want?" Webb demanded as he tossed a hayfork aside and gazed at a rifle resting in the back of an idle wagon.

"I come from Throckmorton," Les announced. "I've got an arrest warrant bearing seven names. Bob Scarlet's at the top of the list."

"Bob ain't here," Emma shouted. "Got himself hurt last night and went down to Albany to see a doctor."

"Be one closer if you boys hadn't shot him!" Dowe yelled. "That's Webb there, Marshal. He's on the list, ain't he?"

"Maybe my little Andy's on it, too," Emma cried. "Why don't you leave us be? Ain't it enough you steal our cattle and fence the range?"

"You'll find no sympathy among us, ma'am," Les countered. "We buried a boy this mornin' not yet full grown, and Dewey's mama before that."

"Others, too," Dowe said bitterly.

"You got no right to come here," Webb argued. "We ain't part of Esperanza."

"I got a county warrant, Webb," Les answered. "And a commission as temporary county sheriff. Your name's high

164

on the first, and mine's on the second. You comin' along peaceful, or do we hog-tie you?''

"Neither one!" Webb shouted as he made a rush for the rifle. He got only halfway before Dowe shot one leg from under him. Webb crawled onward in spite of two warning shots Alf Lowell fired. A third shattered Webb's left wrist.

"Stop!" Dewey yelled as he, too, fired. The bullet struck Webb in the lower side and brought a yelp of pain.

"He's got the rifle!" Dowe shouted, and a half-dozen rifles swung toward Webb Scarlet and fired a single volley. Webb dropped the gun and spun around before dropping to one knee. There was a faint flicker in his eyes. Then, muttering a final curse, Webb Scarlet fell backward in a heap.

The shots drew a rush of riders from beyond the house and a scream from the porch. Emma Scarlet hurried her children inside as three horsemen raced past the barn and disappeared in a second volley of rifle fire. When the smoke drifted away, Willie stared at the horror before him. Two riders lay slumped across their saddles. A third managed to fall off his horse and stumble to Webb's side.

"Which one are you?" Alf asked the limping figure.

"Randolph!" the boy shouted. "That's my brother there you've shot."

"He made the mistake of reaching for that rifle," Les explained.

"Well, he won't make it a second time," Randy said, glaring at the marshal before shifting his eyes to Willie. "You kilt Walt last night and now this."

"He had a chance," Dewey barked. "More'n my ma had."

"Is he on the list?" Alf asked.

"No," Les answered.

"You're hurt, Randy," Willie noted as he dismounted. "Let's have a look at that arm."

"Figure to save me a second time, eh?" Randy cried,

165

stepping back. "Maybe you can shoot Thad next. Or Bob. I only got two brothers left."

"I made you an offer last night," Willie pointed out.

"That was no offer," Randy cried. "Now leave me be! That's my brother you've gone and kilt!"

"Bob'll settle with you for it, too," Emma threatened from the doorway. "Wait and see!"

"These two are dead," Dowe announced after inspecting the bloody corpses of the other riders. "One's Ben Humphrey. You got him on your list. I don't know the other one."

"Aaron Cadwell," Randy said, fighting to steady his quivering limbs. "My cousin. Didn't even have a gun!"

"Should've kept better company," Dowe declared with a grin. "Best take this young one into jail, too, Marshal."

"Don't have a warrant for him," Les explained. "Alf, Joe, you best have a look inside the barn. And the house. Bob was hit last night, all right, and he could be holed up there."

"Stop!" Emma shouted as she lifted a shotgun.

"Ma'am, I got men here eager to kill you," Les said, gazing at Dowe. "You can't mean to leave your youngsters orphans."

The woman stared at the approaching deputies and lowered the gun. As it happened, there was no sign of Bob in either place. Nor did anyone else appear at the house.

"They're sure to be elsewhere," Les finally admitted.

"Sure they are," a weary Randy Scarlet barked as he finally turned his attention to the blood trickling down his arm.

"Did you see his eyes?" Dewey asked when the posse turned back toward Esperanza.

"Yes," Willie muttered. "I guess it really is war now."

When they reached town, Charlie Dowe wasted no time in announcing the posse's exploits. The children stampeded out of the schoolhouse to hear, and others gathered as well.

"We went over to fetch 'em," Dowe boasted, "but they weren't eager to come. So we shot 'em."

"Kilt 'em?" a boy asked.

"Three, includin' that devil Webb. Left Randolph to the care o' Bob's woman. He won't trouble anybody for a while."

"No, but others will," Ellen said as she fought to retrieve her pupils. "They'll be visiting us again now."

"Would seem likely," Les admitted as he dismounted.

The words proved prophetic. Less than an hour later a pillar of thick black smoke rose on the northern horizon. Young Paul Nichols raced out of the schoolhouse closely pursued by two younger brothers.

"Marshal Cobb, it's comin' from my farm!" Paul hollered.

Les grabbed a rifle, called for help, and ran toward his horse. Joe Eagle and Alf Lowell quickly joined the marshal. Dewey and his Uncle Rupert mounted up, as did Willie.

"You sure your pa wasn't goin' to burn cornstalks today?" Les asked a lathered Paul Nichols.

"We use 'em for feed, Marshal," Paul explained. "Miz Trent, will you look after Pete and Jacob?"

Ellen, who had drawn the younger boys to her side, nodded. Paul then mounted a mottled mare and slapped the animal into a gallop. The others followed.

It was the worst kind of riding. Charging down a dusty road and across broken country, with no care to what lay beyond and no plan if trouble waited there. Willie tried to get ahead and cut Paul off, but the fourteen-year-old was chasing hope and pursued by nightmare. For a skinny farm boy on a poor horse, he might have passed for bottled lightning or pure fury.

By the time Paul reached his home, the Esperanza riders were scattered over half a mile. Only Les and Willie were even close, with Dewey and Joe Eagle a hundred yards behind them. A prudent man, especially one who had set as many ambushes as Willie Delamer, would have approached the blazing inferno with caution. But Paul rushed on ahead, and Willie wouldn't leave Les to pursue the boy alone.

"Ma?" Paul screamed as he rolled off his horse. "Pa?" There was no sign of either. Only the boiling flames.

"They got to be in there!" Paul shouted, pointing toward the house."

"Stop it, son!" Les shouted as he jumped from his horse and dove at Paul.

"I got to get to 'em," Paul screamed as Les dragged him from the blazing timbers.

"You don't know they were in there," Les argued. "And if they were, there's nothin' you can do about it."

"Shoulda kilt every one o' them Scarlets!" Charlie Dowe said when he finally arrived. "Paul boy, don't you fret. Your pa told me he planned to take himself a ride down to Albany. Could be he went today."

"Maybe," Paul said, brightening.

"Bob Scarlet was down in Albany," Joe Eagle said, sighing. "Was anybody here besides your mama and papa?"

"Not as I know," Paul replied.

"Somebody was," Eagle said, marching off a ways and pointing to a set of fresh tracks. One rider had come from the river. The others had arrived from the south—from the Clear Fork. Albany.

"Any trace of horses headin' south?" Willie asked.

"Or a wagon?" Paul added.

"Wagon's back o' the barn," Joe explained. "No tracks goin' south."

Paul wriggled free of Les's grasp and walked to the barn. He had a look through the place, then searched the corncrib and hog pens. The porkers rooted as always, and the chickens continued to roost in their coop.

"There goes the back wall," Dowe announced, and Willie watched as the tall ceiling beams gave way as well. He froze in horror as the flames abated. Near what had been the back window three charred lumps huddled together.

"Ma and Pa," Paul said, covering his face and collapsing to his knees.

"Somebody else, too," Les said, grabbing a hoe and making his way to the back wall. He shoved burning timbers to one side or the other until he could reach the bodies. Using the hoe, he pulled them out one at a time.

"That's Miz Nichols," Rupert Hamer mumbled. "I sold her that iron thimble myself."

"It's Pa, too," Paul said as tears streamed down his cheeks. "Or was anyhow."

"Who's the other one?" Alf asked as he helped Les dig a smaller body from the ashes.

"He's near burned up," Dewey said, rushing over to the cover of three tall post oaks before becoming sick.

"Was a boy," Les observed as he tried to clear grit from the body's face. It wasn't possible. Only cinders remained of the legs, arms, and face. There was a bit more of the trunk. And a small knot of melted brass.

"Bullets?" Alf asked.

"No, was a brass cross," Charlie Dowe answered. "Give it to him on his birthday. Lord, you can't be this cruel," the man cried. "It's my Cully!"

"Could be," Paul said, rubbing his eyes. "Cully wasn't at school today."

"Told him to stay home," Dowe muttered. "Didn't want him ridin' off by himself."

"For what it's worth, they were shot first," Eagle said, pointing to the melted plugs of lead liberally peppering the bones.

"Is this what my mama looked like?" Dewey called.

Eagle didn't answer, but his wild gaze betrayed the truth. Dewey stared at his uncle a moment, then turned toward his horse.

"Comin', Paul?" the boy asked. "Mr. Dowe?"

"They'll expect that," Les argued.

"Yes, *they* will!" Dewey shouted, pointing at the corpses.

"Be an ambush waitin' for you," Willie added.

"Forgettin' you got brothers to look after?" Les asked

Paul. Young Nichols hesitated, then dropped to his knees and began pounding the ground.

"They're right, you know," Dowe admitted, turning back toward the house. "And besides, I got a boy to bury."

"Major?" Dewey pleaded. "Wil?"

"I promise you this'll be a debt paid," Willie answered. "But ridin' blind ain't any way to get it done. Been enough dyin' this side of Salt Fork."

"Let's bury the dead and see the Nichols boys looked after," Les suggested. "Then maybe Joe and I'll ride out and have a look at the Scarlet place."

"You'll want company for that," Willie said, staring northward with hate.

"I'm comin', too," Dewey added.

CHAPTER 19

They didn't find Bob Scarlet on the north bank of the Salt Fork. Even Joe Eagle had trouble finding something that wasn't there, and the tracker finally announced Scarlet and his raiders were elsewhere.

"He hasn't finished with the farmers then," Les said, turning his horse southward. "Lord have mercy on them folks."

"He'd better," Dewey added. "Bob Scarlet won't."

He didn't either. There were two more towering columns of smoke south of the river. The nearest marked a pile of blazing fenceposts.

"Was a warnin', Scarlet said," Jonas Kettle explained. "Said sell out or it'd be the house next."

"It would be, too," Rachel Kettle said, clasping her husband's good, right hand. "I heard about the Nichols family. Don't try and argue us out of it, Marshal. We're sellin'."

"Sell, if that's what's on your mind," Willie replied. "Only don't sell to Scarlet. Your land's like a dagger pointed at Esperanza. From here he can run half the people in the county off."

"Who else is buyin'?" Kettle asked.

"I am," Willie answered. "What did he offer?"

171

"Nothin' yet," Kettle confessed. "But he bought the Marcy place for seven hundred."

"I'll pay you a thousand," Willie said. "It's worth more, I'll grant, but it's what I can manage."

"Seems to me it's no different sellin' to you than to Scarlet," Kettle grumbled. "Cowmen, the lot of you."

"Wait for Scarlet's offer then," Willie suggested.

"Jonas!" Rachel complained.

"Can you have the money for us tomorrow?" Kettle asked. "In town? I want to get the children away north soon as possible, what with winter comin' and all."

"Tomorrow at Hamer's Store," Willie said, nodding. "Or we could go down to Throckmorton or Albany and have a lawyer draw up the papers."

"Nichols was goin' to Albany," Kettle pointed out. "We'll be goin' north."

The second fire marked the end of Charlie Dowe. At first Willie suspected the old man might have torched the place himself. Cully's death had struck hard, after all. But just past the blazing house Dowe dangled naked from a white oak limb. SCAR was branded into his hip.

"As good as a signature!" Les declared while Willie and Eagle cut the farmer down.

"He put up a fight," Willie observed, pointing to blood-stains on the ground. Eagle traced one trail past the barn and discovered a corpse.

"Scratch Herb Curry from your list, Les," Eagle called.

After burying Dowe and Curry, they rode eastward. A mile from town they discovered another body beside the road.

"He's on the list, too," Les noted. "Stevenson. I saw him posted in Throckmorton."

"Only two besides Bob Scarlet left," Willie noted. "Together with any newcomers he hired down south."

"Plenty of idle cowboys around Albany," Les grumbled. "Most'd sign on to tear down fences . . . or burn farmers."

"Some," Willie argued. "Not most."

But no matter who did the figuring, there were enough of

them to scare people. The Kettles weren't the only ones eager to leave trouble behind. A steady line of wagons headed north. Many chose to bide their time with relatives in Kansas or Nebraska. Others were eager to sell out and be rid of Texas forever.

Grandma Gunnerson purchased one farm. The others sold to Wil Fletcher.

"You've got yourself a considerable acreage now, Willie," Ellen remarked. "I'm surprised you have that kind of cash."

"I've sold a few horses here lately, and I wired a bank in Colorado for the rest. I have some mining holdings there."

"You're a world of surprises."

"Sure I am," he agreed, grinning.

That next week it seemed the farmers gathered daily in Esperanza to debate their plight. Grandma Gunnerson spoke long and hard, and many others stood firm as well.

"I'm sure staying," Ellen announced. "My husband's buried here. We've paid a high price for this ground."

Young Dewey Hamer spoke of his dead mother, and a defiant Paul Nichols vowed revenge. But many were less certain, and Willie suspected more burnings would send additional wagons north.

"Hold out a little longer, friends," Grandma Gunnerson urged. "Bob Scarlet's runnin' out of brothers . . . and friends. Together we can beat him! Don't let my brave boys die in vain."

Afterward Les drew the old woman and Willie aside.

"Winter's on the wind," the marshal observed. "Scarlet can't stay out in the open forever. He knows we're keepin' a watch on his house, on Emma and the little ones. He's got to act pretty soon. Won't many stand by him when the weather worsens."

"So what do we do?" Mrs. Gunnerson asked.

"Wait," Les told her. "And be ready. If he's got one raid left in him, you know it's sure to be aimed at you, ma'am."

"Or me," Willie suggested. "The Gunnerson place is closer, but so would help be."

"My farm is enclosed with wire now," Grandma said. "And I've hired help. The Nichols boys are there, too, together with Matt and Stef."

"Paul's the only one of any size," Les pointed out. "Might be better for the others to stay in town. Rupe Hamer's offered to put 'em up."

"I may be old, Lester Cobb, and they may be young, but I judge we've got some fight in us," the old woman growled.

"Yes, ma'am," Les agreed, "but I thought you ought to know how it looks. I spoke to my brother. He's sendin' some men to escort Ellen and the little ones down to the Clear Fork."

"How'd you convince her to go?" Willie asked, turning to Les. "I've argued that a hundred times."

"She didn't agree," Les said, shaking his head. "But she's goin' if I have to hog-tie her."

"I'll lend a hand," Willie offered.

"You may have to," Les admitted.

So it was that Willie found himself bidding Ellen farewell yet again. It troubled him some, letting her go, but Travis had brought five men with him to provide escort. The children were excited about visiting their cousins, and Les was visibly relieved to have them out of the line of fire.

"I feel like I'm deserting you," Ellen told Willie before departing. "You and the children in town. I can't teach from the Clear Fork."

"It won't be forever," Willie argued. "And they take a holiday at Christmas anyway."

"Sure," she said, nodding. "Those Scarlets will come for certain now, though. If it wasn't for the children, I'd stay. With us gone you and Lester will both take too many chances. But I can't risk something happening. . . ."

"Nor would I," Willie told her. "We'll put an early end

to all this, and afterward we can maybe find a new start."

"I hope so," she told him.

She kissed him lightly on the cheek, and he held her a long minute. Then the little ones said their good-byes. Anne clung to him a moment, and Billy rubbed a tear from his eye.

"Be careful, Uncle Wil," he said somberly. "You and Dewey save some deer for us to hunt."

"Sure," Willie agreed.

"Be quiet hereabouts with them gone," Dewey said, stepping over beside Willie and waving farewell.

"Truth is, I wish you'd go with 'em," Willie told the young man. "Or stay with your uncle in Esperanza."

"No, I gone and growed whiskers," Dewey declared, rubbing his chin. "I'll be stayin'. I shoot fair, too, remember?"

"I do, and I won't say you're not welcome, Dewey. But it's a bitter winter feelin' freezes the heart when you kill men. And we'll be doin' that soon."

Willie expected a band of riders to gallop up to the house that very night. Even with Dewey, Les, and the two deputies, it would be a challenge to hold off an attack. But as it happened, there was but one rider that evening. Fourteen-year-old Thad Scarlet appeared after supper.

"What's on your mind, Thad?" Willie asked, cautiously stepping outside to face the boy.

"I come to talk to Miz Trent," Thad explained. "Brought an offer."

"You'd best deal with me now."

"Bought her out, too, did you? We heard about your dealin's. Plan to ranch here yourself, I guess. Well, we got first claim as Bob sees it. We'll see you don't lose on the sale, though. Pay you five hundred dollars besides."

"No, I plan to stay a long time, Thad. Run horses. I could still use a hand or two. Change of work might spell a longer life."

"We had this talk," Thad grumbled.

"That how it is then?"

"I'll be back, you know, Major. Ain't any debts owed now."

"No, just friends to kill."

"Yeah, there's that," the boy confessed, softening just a moment. "For what it's worth, I thought some on your offer. But I got to be who I am. I'd never get used to a hundred different names."

The words stung, but Willie read no malice on Thad's face. That was good. Willie wanted to recall the boy he'd fished from Pease River, even if there were few hints of childhood left in Thad's voice or manner.

"Figure tomorrow?" Les asked, appearing in the doorway as Thad rode away.

"That's how I'd do it," Willie replied. "Bob Scarlet'll be on us as soon as Thad passes view."

Les trotted to the barn to alert Joe Eagle and Alf Lowell, but the deputies were already bundled in their heavy buffalo-hide coats and wielding rifles.

Bob Scarlet led the charge himself. The rancher was charmed indeed, for though he winced with pain from his earlier wounds, no bullet found him as he sped toward the low stone wall.

His companions weren't so lucky. Les dropped one rider at a hundred yards, and Lowell shot a second. Dewey fired furiously into the shadowy line, but his bullets were aimed low and mostly struck horseflesh.

Willie waited. And waited. Only when the riders loomed close did he open fire. The Winchester then spit death with rare fury. There was no accounting made now, as horsemen and crouching defenders tangled in a wild melee. Joe Eagle simply went mad, firing a pistol in one hand and slashing with a bowie knife held in the other.

"Get that roof goin'!" Bob shouted.

Willie spied a figure dashing toward the house with a flaming tinder bundle. He started that way, but a shot tore through his leg, and he fell.

"Major!" Dewey called, but Willie ignored the shout.

Instead he limped after the would-be arsonist. As the shadow climbed the woodpile, Willie fired twice.

"Bob?" Thad called, dropping the burning bundle as he toppled from the woodpile. Willie rushed over to stomp out the flames and found himself staring at Thad's pale face.

"Leave the pistol be," Willie said as he kicked a shiny Remington pistol away. "Hurt bad?"

"Bad enough," Thad said, turning his head to peer at two large holes in his side. "I'd've made a poor excuse for a wrangler, Major. Not much of a night rider, either."

Willie heard movement behind him, and he whirled in time to see Dewey Hamer blast Bob Scarlet from his horse.

"Shot by a fool kid," Bob managed to mutter before Dewey fired a second bullet through his forehead.

"It's over now," Willie said, turning back to Thad. But the boy's eyes stared blankly at the stars overhead.

The shooting continued for a quarter hour before the last two horsemen raced off into the night.

"Everybody in one piece?" Les called out. "Alf? Joe?" The deputies answered.

"Dewey, you did just fine," Les added as he stepped past Bob Scarlet's corpse and knelt beside Willie. "Bad?"

"Missed the bone, I think," Willie said, pressing his hands against the bloody mess that was his left calf.

"Help me get him inside, Dewey," Les said. "Ole fool just can't get through a fight without gettin' shot."

Willie tried to laugh, but pain surged up his leg, and he winced.

"You'll be mighty sorry Jack's dead," Les added when he helped Willie onto the kitchen table and set a kerosene lamp alongside him. "I got no gift for carvin' bullets."

"Then find me a bottle," Willie urged.

"No, you'll pass out soon's I start," Les said, laughing to himself as he ran the blade of a kitchen knife under the lantern's flame. Les then touched the fiery knife to the wound, and Willie screamed. Waves of pain engulfed him, and he lost consciousness.

CHAPTER 20

Willie awoke to find himself sprawled on Billy Trent's slat bed. Cloth bandages wrapped his left leg from knee to ankle. He felt a bit feverish, but otherwise he was fine. His eyes sharpened into focus, and he gazed at the bright sunshine streaming through the window.

"I was beginning to think you'd sleep forever," Ellen said as she knelt beside him.

"You got here mighty fast," he grumbled. "Can't be much past ten o'clock. Called school off again, did you?"

"Was needed here," she explained. "As to getting here fast, I didn't hear about the raid till yesterday afternoon. It took the rest of the day to convince Trav to bring me back here."

"But it was just last night . . ."

"You've been out of your head two days," she explained. "And alive, no thanks to Lester's doctoring. If Joe Eagle hadn't opened up your wound, you'd be shy a leg by now. It did a proper job of festering."

"Didn't know Joe was a medicine man," Willie muttered.

"I suspect he can do most anything when the mood strikes him. I wouldn't discount prayer, either. Most of Throckmorton County's mentioned you these past few days. Grandma Gunnerson came by awhile back and left you a peach pie. Nearly everybody else has sent something by way of thanks. Of course, Les claims most of the credit. He and Dewey Hamer. Did that child really kill Bob Scarlet?''

''As I recall,'' Willie said, sighing. ''How's he holdin' up?''

''Sour. He told me this morning you warned him it wouldn't set with him like he thought. He looks older, I think. Hard like you were when you came home from the war.''

''Not that hard, I hope.''

''Well, maybe it will pass with him. He's been out working those black ponies. I noticed him almost smiling after he was thrown the last time.''

''Maybe a good bounce or two will shake the sorrow from him.''

''Maybe,'' she whispered. ''Do you think you can eat something? I've got some broth heated.''

''I'll try,'' he agreed.

''And there are some people eager to see you. Ready for company?''

''If you'll move that blanket over so it covers a bit more of me. Wouldn't want anybody's modesty bothered.''

''I don't think that will be much of a problem with these visitors,'' Ellen said, laughing.

She was right. First in were Travis and his boy Mike. They chatted a while about horses, asked how the leg felt, and shared a humorous tale or two. Then Billy Trent brought in a bowl of broth.

''Mama said not to eat it too fast, Uncle Wil,'' the ten-year-old cautioned. ''Maybe Uncle Travis'll help you sit. Eating soup's not so easy flat on your back.''

''You sure it's safe to bring the children back?'' Willie asked Travis.

''I expect so,'' Travis answered. ''Les rode out to the Scarlet place yesterday, but they'd cleared out. On toward nightfall there were some others out that way. Burned the place to the ground.''

"Well, you understand how folks'd be bitter.''

"And generous at the same time. You've had an army of visitors.''

"So Ellie's said.''

"Young Dewey's lookin' after the horses just fine,'' Travis explained as he rose to his feet. "We'll bring the others along next week. I figure you'll be stayin' on here.''

"Sure he will,'' Billy answered. "Everybody knows that.''

"Everybody?'' Willie asked wearily.

"It's a fact,'' Mike declared. "Cobb and Ellis chattered away like magpies the whole way here, sayin' how you'd teach 'em to ride and hunt deer and all sorts of foolishness. Even Annie's got herself figurin' to ride bareback 'fore summer.''

"I made no promises,'' Willie objected.

"It's not us you got to argue with,'' Travis said, grinning. "And nobody I know's won an argument from Ellie since she was ten. Even then she threw the both of us in the river!''

"Yeah, she did,'' Willie remembered. "Thanks for stoppin' in, Trav. You, too, Mike. I know you got work waitin' and family of your own to tend.''

"You get that leg to movin' soon, eh, Willie?'' Travis urged. "It'll stiffen on you.''

"Seems like you said the same thing back in Corinth the spring of '62.''

"Was as true then as it is now.''

"I'll heed good advice every time,'' Willie said, clasping Travis's hand. Then he devoted himself to emptying the soup bowl.

After swallowing the last of the broth, Willie swung his leg off the end of the bed and painfully rested it on the floor. As the burning sensation passed, he managed to sit up on the edge of the bed.

"Figure you can find something I can use for a crutch?" Willie asked Billy.

"Papa kept a couple of forked cottonwood limbs around," the boy answered. "I'll fetch one."

When Billy scampered off to locate the crutch, Ellis and Cobb slipped into the room with their little sister Anne. The three younger Trents studied Willie's tired features with worried gazes.

"Figure I'll live?" Willie finally asked them.

"You better," Cobb answered. "We got a lot of holes in the barn to mend, and three broken windows in the house."

"Always bones to knit and holes to mend," Willie said sadly. "And graves to dig."

"Uncle Les saw to the graves," Cobb explained. "You got the only wound needs mendin'. Mama says it'll come 'round now she's doin' the doctorin'."

"I expect she's right," Willie told them.

Billy reappeared with the crutch, and Willie used it to rise from the bed. He thought to hobble outside, but Billy blocked the path.

"Best get you some trousers first," Billy observed. "It's turned cold. A nightshirt won't do much warming."

"Nor covering either," Cobb added with a snicker.

Ellis escorted Anne outside, and the boys set about helping him dress. In short order they got him into a flannel shirt and some overalls. Billy managed to pull stockings over Willie's bare feet, and they got the right boot on, too. The left was too much for them, for Willie's foot was swollen and too tender to be forced.

"Thanks, boys," Willie said as he used the crutch to step away from the bed. Then he struggled through the door and on to the porch.

For several minutes Willie chatted with Alf Lowell and Joe Eagle. To them had fallen the dreadful task of burying the dead.

"Put 'em in a common hole down by the river," Eagle explained. " 'Cept for the boy, Thad, and ole Bob. Figured

181

their people might call for them. Dewey scratched out a grave for the two of 'em yesterday, just below your cabin under the oaks.''

"Any sign of trouble?" Willie asked.

"We rode around some, but it's finished, what with the house burned and all," Lowell declared. "Nobody to pay the bills now Bob's gone. I thought I might make the county an offer on the land. Les says Scarlet never held title."

"Figure to turn your hand to ranching, eh?" Willie asked.

"Lot of cows hereabouts. Funny, but I hear some of the farmers talkin' about turnin' to livestock raisin', too. Guess they had their fill o' breakin' rocks and scratchin' out cornfields."

"That'd be a fine note!" Eagle grumbled. "If they fight a war with the cowmen, win, and then turn to it themselves."

"Life's strange that way, though," Willie observed. He thought to recount some puzzlement from the past, but Dewey raced over on his buckskin, pointing wildly at a swirl of dust rising from the road.

"Fetch me a rifle," Willie urged.

"You sit yourself down and leave us to handle this," Alf scolded. "Like as not some farmers bringin' you another pie."

It wasn't, though. Willie knew that much from the panic etched in Dewey's forehead.

"Willie?" Ellen called from the door when he crutched his way down the steps and joined Joe Eagle near the stone wall.

"Get yourself inside and watch the little ones," he urged. "Keep low."

"It's the Scarlets!" Dewey exclaimed as he caught his breath.

"He's right," Les announced as a wagon emerged from the dust. Randy Scarlet rode alongside, one arm in a sling and a funeral pallor flooding his face.

"Best hold up there, Scarlet!" Les shouted, and Emma halted the wagon. Randy rode on ahead a step or two, then stopped.

"Didn't come for trouble," Randy declared, opening his empty palms. "Figure Emma and me brought the little ones on a raid? Maybe Emmett there or Andrew has a rifle hidden away."

"What do you want?" Les demanded.

"I had two brothers kilt here," Randy said bitterly. "One of the fellows that wasn't told us that much before he stole what money was left. We started out to see about 'em yesterday, but some farmers set our house on fire, and we turned back to try and save somethin'. Were too late. Anyhow, I was hopin' you could tell me where you put Bob . . . and Thad."

"Kept 'em for you to tend till yesterday," Dewey said, softening his hard stare. "But even this time of year they get to smellin', and . . . the birds and all. . . . I buried 'em in the oaks above the river."

"Thad was fond of shade," Willie noted. "As I recall."

"Was," Randy agreed. "Weighs on you some, I see. Thad wouldn't hold it against you."

"Wish he'd taken me up on my offer," Willie said, swallowing hard. "Would've made a fair wrangler."

"Sure, he would have. But he had his road to travel. Deemed it a duty to go along, even though his heart wasn't in it."

"And Bob?" Willie asked.

"The war twisted his insides all up," Emma said, losing a touch of her harsh gaze. "Some'll think him a murderer and a killer, but he saw worse before he passed his fifteenth birthday than any man alive should ever see. Soured him."

If she was expecting sympathy from the Trents or Les Cobb, she was disappointed. Willie judged she hadn't sought anything. Was only offering a reason for the madness.

"So what'll you do now?" Willie asked.

"Ride west," Randy explained. "No place for us here. That's for certain. I'm all that's left, and that's not much. But the boys'll grow in time. Maybe we'll find somethin' better over the next hill."

"I hope so," Willie said, nodding.

"I'll show you the graves," Dewey offered as he turned toward the river. The Scarlets turned to follow. With them went a cloud of sadness.

As the wagon rumbled back toward the river, Ellen stepped out of the house and wrapped an arm around Willie's waist. He smiled at her, and she rested her head against his cheek.

"Guess that means my work's at an end," Les announced. He plucked the star from his vest and tossed it to Ellen.

"Lester?" she gasped.

"Got a pretty little gal waitin' for me in Kansas," Les explained. "Wants a gold ring for Christmas. Says she wants twenty kids that look like me. Figured I might oblige her."

"Well, you never said a word!" she complained. "But why give it to me? Alf ought to . . ."

"I'm goin' into the cattle business," Lowell insisted.

"I'd take it, ma'am," Joe Eagle announced, "but folks here in Texas aren't apt to want an Indian marshal. Besides, I promised Dewey I'd catch up on some huntin'."

"I know a man who might work out," Les said, turning to Willie. "He's had a hair of experience, and the people would support him. Once old Joe finishes emptyin' the bottoms of deer, he might sign on as deputy. Well, Wil?"

"The badge fits well enough," Ellen said as she pinned it to his shirt. "A lawman needs roots, of course. A place he belongs."

"Everybody needs that," Willie confessed as she tightened her grip on him.

"You won't be riding off this time, will you?"

"No need, Ellie," he said, kissing her forehead. "I guess this is as close to home as I'm apt to get."

Billy ran over and touched the shiny sliver of tin. Cobb followed, and Ellis helped Anne over as well.

"Yes, you're home, all right," Ellen declared. "We all are."

ABOUT THE AUTHOR

G. Clifton Wisler comes by his interest in the West naturally. Born in Oklahoma and raised in Texas, he discovered early on a fascination for the history of the region. His first novel, *My Brother, the Wind*, received a nomination for the American Book Award in 1980. Among the many others that have followed are *Thunder on the Tennessee*, winner of the Western Writers of America Spur Award for Best Western Juvenile Book of 1983; *Winter of the Wolf*, a Spur finalist in 1982; and Delamer Westerns *The Trident Brand*, *Starr's Showdown*, *Purgatory*, *Abrego Canyon*, *The Wayward Trail*, *Sweetwater Flats*, *Sam Delamer*, and *Clear Fork*. *Among the Eagles*, a Delamer Western, was honored by the Western Writers as best original paperback of 1989. In addition to his writing, Wisler frequently speaks to school groups and conducts writing clinics. He lives in Plano, Texas, where he is active in Boy Scouts.